Knitbone Pepper
Ghost Dog

Knitbone Pepper
Ghost Dog

By Claire Barker Illustrated by Ross Collins

Contents

Chapter 1

Dog-gone

The first thing that struck Knitbone Pepper about death was that Heaven wasn't up to much.

There weren't any squirrels, or sausage sandwiches, or delicious bones, or even a single squeaky ball. Instead it seemed to be full of stripy socks, jumpers and the smell of washing powder. It was also quite dark. There were supposed to be sparkly lights, not spangly tights.

Knitbone was definitely dead, because he could remember the dying part quite clearly...

Yesterday, he had felt really old and tired and fed up. So fed up in fact, that he couldn't even get out of bed. Then the nice vet who smelled of cats and biscuits came, and everybody's eyes started leaking.

The Peppers sat in a small, sad circle, passing around tissues, wiping their eyes and blowing their noses – so much so that Knitbone hoped they weren't coming down with something.

Lord Pepper, sniffing loudly, carefully tucked Knitbone's favourite toy rabbit (Floppy Bernard) beneath his doggy chin and Lady Pepper gently squeezed his paw. Then Winnie – lovely Winnie – kneeled down and stroked his ears in the special way he liked. She came very close, her warm tears sploshing onto his nose, and whispered, "Thank you for being the best, most special, most perfect dog in all the world. Sleep tight, Knitbone Pepper.

We love you so much. Goodbye, goodbye…"

Then, SHAZAM! He was as dead as a doorknob. Actually it was surprisingly nice, because one minute everything hurt, and the next it didn't. In fact, he felt great, like a puppy again, all bendy and WOW!

He had expected to go to Heaven straight away, via angel wings and twanging harps. He had seen it on those Saturday morning cartoons, sitting next to Winnie, as she crunched toast and he munched dog biscuits. It looked painless, well organized and quite straightforward.

But it wasn't straightforward for Knitbone Pepper. It was dead complicated.

Knitbone carefully inspected a nurse's costume in a dark corner. It had a catapult in the pocket and chocolate down the front. He gave it a sniff and was relieved to discover he was shut inside Winnie's wardrobe, not in Heaven after all.

He picked his way through a forest of tangled wire coat hangers and nudged open the door with his nose. Outside, the air felt cool and still as his gaze fell onto the bed in the corner of the room. Hunched up beneath its rainbow patchwork cover was the outline of a familiar shape.

Immediately Knitbone's heart looped the loop and his tail began to whoosh like a windscreen wiper. Oh, MAD love! Wonderful, marvellous, amazing, *Winnie Pepper*. He loved her more than all the bicycle wheels, frisbees and cowpats in the world. They had made a promise to be BFFs: Best Friends Forever. Like tea and toast, fish and chips, strawberries and cream; Winnie and Knitbone were made for each other. He scampered over and watched her for a blissful moment, his head patiently resting on her bedcover as he thought about how pleased she was going to be when she saw him. It would be the best surprise EVER. There must have been some sort of mistake.

Maybe he wasn't dead after all or, at worst, only a *bit* dead. Whatever had happened, it didn't matter because any minute soon Winnie would wake up and smile and say, "*There* you are, Knitbone, you good boy!" and everything would be the same as before.

He licked her cheek. Normally her face tasted of peppermint toothpaste or bubblegum, but today she tasted different: strange and salty. He snuffled at her hair. It smelled sad. His gaze drifted down to her hand. In it rested a photograph of a knee-high dog with wonky ears and toffee-coloured, scrubbing-brush fur. He was wearing a pirate hat, perched at a cheeky angle. This dog certainly wasn't a pedigree, more of a doggy jumble, but his eyes twinkled like the brightest stars. "Ooh, look," Knitbone woofed cheerfully. "It's me!"

There was a knock at the door. Winnie's mum came in and sat on the bed. She looked sad and her eyes were all puffy. Maybe she did have a cold after all. "Wake up, Winnie," she whispered. "It's time for school."

Normally Winnie was like a fizzing firework, springing out of bed. But not today. Today she just rolled over and faced the wall.

Knitbone bounded around madly at first, in case it was a game. He loved games. Then he realized it wasn't, so he stopped and did a bit of happy panting instead. Still Winnie continued to face the wall, ignoring her mother's coaxing. "Well, I can see this is a job for a dog," he sighed, squeezing in front of Winnie's mum. "Never fear, Knitbone's here! Come on now, Winnie, wake up. Stop messing about."

He plonked his paw heavily on Winnie's leg and nudged her with his wet nose. She didn't seem to notice, so he did it again, this time a little more firmly.

"Winnie, it's *me* – vitamin D! Geddit? D for

13

Dog? Ha ha! No? Oh. Come on. If you get up now
there will be time to play a game before the school
bus comes. I want to have a go at 'Jump the Piano'
because, guess what? I'm feeling much better today,
look!" He pranced about in front of her like a loon,
trying to catch her eye. "WINNIE, LOOK!" But
Winnie just curled into a ball and pulled a pillow
over her head as if she hadn't heard a thing.

Knitbone had a peculiar feeling. It wasn't a very
nice one. Then a Bad Thought occurred to him.

Knitbone Pepper wasn't very good at maths
(he was, after all, a dog), but even he had to
admit that:

$$Dead + still\ here = Ghost$$

He looked down at his paws. They *were* a bit
see-through, now he came to think about it. If he
had to describe them, he would say they looked
as if they were made out of wispy cotton wool.

Standing next to Winnie's dressing table, he noticed that whilst the teddy bear, the piggybank and the alarm clock were reflected in the mirror, he wasn't. The reality of the situation hit him over the head like a saucepan – *CLAAAANG!*

Knitbone's tail drooped and panic began to rise in his chest. "No, no, NO*OOOOO!* NOT A GHOST! I can't be – this can't be happening!" He wailed and howled as loudly as he could. "PEPPERS, LOOK! IT'S ME, KNITBONE!"

Winnie was eventually persuaded out of bed in her nightdress and led downstairs, Knitbone following close behind. "LISTEN, I'M STILL HERE – I'M STILL PART OF THE FAMILY!" Winnie and Lady Pepper didn't so much as glance backwards.

Down in the kitchen, Knitbone was in something of a panic. Dying had gone very badly wrong. He was neither here nor there – he was somewhere in-between. He hid under the big kitchen table for a while and tried to calm down by breathing deeply and thinking about safe things like tartan blankets and dog biscuits.

After a while he felt brave enough to come out. He sat next to Winnie's chair, staring super-hard at her whilst tears plopped rhythmically into her cornflakes. His trusting doggy heart had to believe that Winnie would make everything alright again. Surely any moment now she would look up from her breakfast and announce, "Oh, THERE you are,

Knitbone!" After all, Winnie was the cleverest, most wonderful person in the world, so she was bound to figure it out, sooner or later.

But she didn't look up. Not that day, nor the next, nor even the next.

Chapter 2

There's No Place Like Home

There had been Peppers living at Starcross Hall (Bartonshire, England) for 904 years precisely. The house snuggled into the surrounding countryside, undisturbed by the modern world, fast asleep and dreaming of times past. Birds nested in the eaves and shiny green ivy threaded its way through the patched roof. Built by their forebears, stone upon stone, the family were as much a part of Starcross Hall as the snails on the walls and the moss on the doorstep.

The Peppers were the soul of the place, and the place was in their souls. To put it simply – if your last name was Pepper, Starcross spelled H-O-M-E.

Once upon a time, Starcross Hall had been a very impressive stately home, ringing with the sound of banquets and masked balls, roaring battle cries and triumphant trumpets. These days though, Starcross was just a rickety old wreck at the end of a bumpy dirt track. Ferns grew out of the chimneys, cobwebs hung from the rafters and, in a high wind, important bits fell off. But it was a very happy home, nonetheless.

Unlike their ancestors, Lord and Lady Pepper were as poor as poets. However, they *did* carry on the ancient Pepper tradition of being completely crackers. When they weren't tending the bees or digging up vegetable "treasures" in the bramble-tangled garden, their time was devoted to being loopy and cheerfully parading around in big hats without a care in the world.

The Peppers owned an enormous collection of antique hats, filling trunks and wardrobes to overflowing. These had been handed down, generation after generation, and as a result, the Peppers had an impressive array of headgear to suit every imaginable occasion. They owned tricornes, turbans, top hats, fedoras, fezzes, tiaras, skullcaps, bowlers, berets, bonnets festooned in rainbow ribbons, balaclavas, boaters, bearskins... and even a spectacular warrior's helmet with horns. The Peppers simply didn't have the time or inclination to be sensible and laughed a lot.

The higgledy-piggledy state of Starcross Hall suited their unusual family to a T; swivel-eyed chickens nested in the airing cupboard and black bats flapped up and down the corridors. Generations of long dead Peppers smiled down from their huge portraits, overseeing all manner of strange and wonderful shenanigans.

One day the house might be filled with the sound of yodelling practice and the next the whole family would be taking part in the Starcross Banister Helter-skelter Championships. No two days were the same and it was completely brilliant.

Lord and Lady Pepper's heads were full of pressing questions like, "*Do penguins have knees?*" and "*Why doesn't glue stick to the inside of the bottle?*" Therefore there was nobody to complain about the noise and general chaos. This meant

that Winnie and Knitbone were free to do whatever they felt like, whether it was dressing up in faded silk turbans and flying goggles, bowling in the ballroom or digging for treasure in the conservatory. No game was too loud, too mad or too messy for Starcross Hall. It was their own unique adventure playground and dogs were *definitely* allowed in. It was the sort of place where a dog would be welcome to drink out of the toilet whenever he wanted. In a nutshell, it was perfect and the Peppers wanted it to stay the same always, for ever and a day.

Knitbone felt this from the moment he arrived, just before lunchtime, several years earlier...

Lady Pepper had found herself developing an alarming taste for unusual foods. She put it down to a "naturally adventurous spirit", but Lord Pepper suspected it was more to do with her growing baby bump. Some days she wanted peanut butter, other days she thought that coal sounded delicious. On this particular day, Lady Pepper desperately wanted beetroot and she was convinced that she had seen some amongst the tangled undergrowth of the vegetable garden.

So, after donning a striking Sherlock Holmes hat, and armed with pruning shears, Lady Pepper marched outside and began the hunt. Not put off by the jungle of weeds, she enthusiastically pulled out nettles, brambles and thistles, loudly singing a song about delicious ruby-red beetroot.

But to her dismay, all her work was for nothing. For underneath was no beetroot, just a patch of floppy-leaved knitbone plants. She was disappointed at first, but then an intriguing thought occurred: what if knitbone leaves tasted better than beetroot? Lady Pepper bent down, grasped around the base of one of the plants and, to her horror, her fingers touched something warm and fat! If this wasn't bad enough, whatever it was *licked her hand*! Recoiling to the other side of the vegetable patch, she hoped it wasn't a giant, disgusting mutant slug. *Yeeuch*. However, because

the Peppers had always been a curious bunch,
she decided to investigate.

On parting the furry knitbone leaves, she
uncovered, to her astonishment,
something remarkable
sitting underneath.
It wasn't a ginormous
slug at all, but a
soft brown
puppy.
Big shiny
eyes gazed
up at her
as if to say, "I've been waiting here for *ages*.
Where have you been?"

How he got there, nobody knew, but the
Peppers believed that sometimes marvellous
and unexpected things just *happened*. And as
far as Lady Pepper was concerned, he had arrived
at *precisely* the right moment. She picked him up,

popped him snugly into her apron pocket and brought him inside, forgetting all about the beetroot. A few weeks after this unearthing, a distant aunt had commented that Knitbone was a "funny sort of name for a dog". Had they thought of calling him Rover? Or Pooch? Lord and Lady Pepper had simply smiled, adjusting the baby bonnet on his head, because they knew that Knitbone was no ordinary dog. And a special dog needed a special name. So Knitbone he stayed.

Knitbone was "Starcross home-grown"; there was no other place in the world for him. Here he became an expert on scooting and spinning across the worn, wooden floorboards. Here he chased sooty crows up and down the chimneys, and here he learned how to howl mournfully until Lord and Lady P let him onto their bed. He knew the best sort of antique chair leg to chew and where the warmest shafts of honeyed sunlight fell through the criss-crossed windows. Everything Knitbone knew, he knew because of Starcross.

Before the summer was out, to Knitbone's delight, a laughing baby Pepper appeared. They named her Winifred Clementine Violet Araminta Pepper (known as "Winnie" for short). Winnie was another Starcross home-grown, so they were like two peas in a pod.

Knitbone loved all of the Peppers. He loved Lord Pepper's tendency to drop his dinner under the table and he loved Lady Pepper's frisbee practice in the kitchen. They were both very, very good at scratching his tummy.

But his favourite Pepper was undoubtedly Winnie. He'd taken care of her since she was a baby; picking up things that she dropped from her high chair and keeping her face clean of sticky things like ice cream and ketchup. She rode on his back and he lay on her lap.

She grew and grew, until the day came that she had to go to school. Knitbone, not really understanding what was going on, missed her all day. To make up for it, he was given the special job of walking her up the old lane to the Starcross bus stop and collecting her again at home time. This made him feel much better.

Lord and Lady P, Winnie, the hats, the echoing corridors and the cosy fireplaces, the tangled gardens and the old lane – it was Knitbone's entire world. But now, owing to some inconvenient dying, that world had been turned upside down.

Chapter 3
Wonderful Winnie Pepper

Three days of hard thinking and anxious stick-chewing later, Knitbone came to a decision. As he saw it, the Peppers were his family, and families stick together. Blood was thicker than custard, or something along those lines. So (in a move that was not dissimilar to sticking his paws in his ears and going tra-lalalalalalala), Knitbone simply decided to ignore being dead and carry on as if nothing had happened.

The next morning bright and early, Knitbone climbed out of the wardrobe, licked his paws and smoothed down his eyebrows. Then he went straight to the courtyard, sat down and waited patiently. It was a school day and he was ready to resume duties.

Eventually Winnie came out, wiping her eyes and blowing her nose. Knitbone had a plan; all he needed to do was draw attention to himself. He was going to *make* her notice him. How hard could it be?

Winnie opened the creaky iron gates and Knitbone scooted after her. "Goodness, I'm so nippy now, *zip*, ZOOM, *zip*!" he giggled, circling Winnie excitedly. "Look, Winnie, LOOK!"

Winnie sighed miserably and began the trudge up the lane to the bus stop.

Trotting along in the sunshine and hoping to jog her memory, Knitbone chattered away. "*Winnie*, do you remember the time I got my head stuck in the pickle jar and you said I looked like an astronaut? Come on! You must remember that…"

The school bus pulled up and the doors opened with a heavy sigh. "What about the time we saved the baby bird?" he called after her as she clambered onto the bus. The doors closed. "Winnie! Winnie! Listen!"

But she just stared glumly out of the window as the bus trundled away, getting smaller and smaller, disappearing along with Knitbone's hopes. He lay down and howled.

It was a long wait until home time. Knitbone sat patiently at the bus stop, his gaze fixed on the horizon, until the school bus finally came back over the hill and drew up by him. The doors slid open and Winnie popped out, book bag flying and coat undone.

"Hello, Winnie! It's me!" Knitbone woofed, full of hope. "Did you have a good day?"

Winnie marched down the lane, head down,
plaits flip-flapping in the wind, completely
unaware of the ghost dog plodding sadly at
her heel.

Winnie had always been a happy-go-lucky girl.
Everyone said so. She was the sort of girl who
could do a perfect cartwheel, pick a daisy halfway

round and present it to you at the end with a
rosy-cheeked grin. She loved penguins, cheese
sandwiches and running like the wind. Above all,
she was kind. Suffice to say, if a worm was stuck
in a puddle, you could guarantee that Winnie
Pepper would take the time to stop and save it.

She had a natural talent for seeing the best in
things. For example, when Lady Pepper's woolly

bobble hat shrunk in the wash, Winnie had the idea of turning it into a tea cosy. When Lady P shrunk it even more, she then congratulated her mother on creating the most perfect egg warmer. When Lord Pepper got tangled in the curtains and pulled an antique curtain pole down, snapping it in two, Winnie announced it was time for a sword fight. They had a marvellous time, duelling all afternoon with sticks and cushions.

When the roof of the chicken barn collapsed, Winnie declared it to be the ideal place to grow pumpkins. She grew them until they were big and fat and then sold them in a little home-made shop at the end of the lane. With the money she collected, she bought Knitbone a smart new collar with pictures of pumpkins on it, which he liked very much. Winnie had a wonderful way of making gloomy situations seem brighter.

But when Knitbone died, everything fell into shadow. She put the collar away in a box, and placed it deep inside her dressing table drawer. People gave her advice and patted her on the head. Her teacher, the school bus driver, even the lady at the corner shop, all said things like, "never mind" and that "time heals everything". The postman said it was probably best to get a new puppy as soon as possible and gave her a sympathetic wink.

Winnie listened politely, nodding and swallowing her misery. But all the time she knew that *her* dog wasn't like other dogs. Knitbone Pepper had been the BEST dog in the world. Simple as sunshine and plain as pie crust. If they'd known him like she did, they'd understand. But they hadn't, so they couldn't.

Lord and Lady Pepper were utterly heartbroken about Knitbone, of course, but they weren't the sort to talk about difficult things.

Knitbone had been the one who Winnie turned to when she felt sad. His warm fur and understanding expression made everything better. He even had a special trick where he fetched a hanky when she cried. That always made her smile and cheered her up straight away. Because of this, she never got cross when he did naughty things. She let him lick her face and only insisted on bathing him if he had done something truly unmentionable with poo.

At the end of the school day, Knitbone was always waiting to play with her as soon as she got off the bus, tail wagging madly and tongue hanging out. Time unravelled before them like an endless ribbon of adventure and their free-range friendship seemed guaranteed. All her life, Winnie had never known what it was to be lonely.

Now everything was different, everything was all wrong – *Winnie Pepper* was all wrong. She pushed open the big, wooden front door and stepped into the hallway. "Oh, Knitbone Pepper," she sighed as she hung her bag on the coat-stand. "Where are you when I need you?"

Chapter 4

"For the Attention of Ye Dead"

Dejected, Knitbone followed Winnie up the stairs, and realized it was time to face facts – he'd been rubbed out like a wonky pencil line. It was hopeless. No matter how hard he tried, clearly Winnie was clueless that he was still by her side. He was fed up with trying to put a brave face on things – the truth was that being dead was totally pants. He sighed a big, sad sigh and clambered into the wardrobe. Here he circled round a couple of times, trampled a nest out of

Winnie's spangly tights and drifted off to sleep, hoping it would be for a *very* long time…

In the still of the night, Knitbone was unexpectedly woken by hushed curses on the other side of the wardrobe door. He sat up, frozen in the dark, holding his breath and too scared to move. Some of the words sounded quite rude.

To his horror, a crumpled envelope was shoved roughly under the wardrobe door. Knitbone hugged his paws close to his ears, squeezed his eyes tight shut and sang his happy song ("Limpy Squirrel") until he was sure "they" had gone away. Then he threw out Floppy Bernard, his toy rabbit, as a sacrifice – because you can't be too careful.

Nothing seemed to happen, so Knitbone eventually pushed the door open and cautiously peered out into the room. A sliver of cold moonlight poured through the gap in Winnie's curtains and spilled across the bedroom carpet.

Winnie lay fast asleep, snuggled under her covers like a snoozing caterpillar. He peered down at the envelope by his feet. Dogs can see rather well in the dark, so, despite the inkiness of the night, he could make out the words quite clearly.

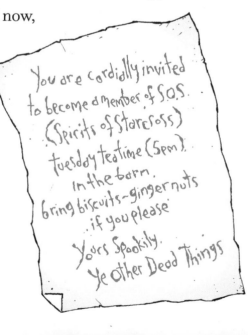

for the attention of Ye Dead

He looked at it for a while and then gave it a bit of a lick.

He sniffed it – it smelled interesting, like gingery crumbs. Knitbone supposed he *was* "Ye Dead" now, so he turned the envelope over, and pulled out the paper carefully with his teeth.

You are cordially invited to become a member of S.O.S. (Spirits of Starcross) tuesday teatime (5pm). In the barn. bring biscuits – gingernuts if you please

Yours Spookily.
Ye Other Dead Things

Knitbone Pepper stared at the invitation.
This raised lots of issues, not least of all the fact he
could now read.

Secondly, it meant that somebody knew he was
here. And if somebody knew he was here, then he
wasn't alone after all! This was big, *big* news. Were
they people ghosts? If they were, then surely they
would be Peppers too? Maybe they needed a dog? He
tried his wag just in case. Yes, it still worked. *Phew.*

His heart leaped and his thoughts raced.
Feeling more alive than he had in a while (well,
for a few days at least), Knitbone didn't know
whether to be pleased or scared. In the end he
decided to be pleased as, honestly, dead things
probably didn't need to be scared of anything.
(When he was alive he had been scared of lots of
things. He now realized that he should have been
more concerned about being dead and a lot less
frightened of the vacuum cleaner.)

The next day, Knitbone enthusiastically explored the pantry. A pack of ginger biscuits sat on the top shelf. Teetering precariously on a chair and a pile of cookery books, he managed to roll them off the edge into a basket of laundry – "Bingo!"

As he balanced the packet in his jaws and trotted back to the safety of the wardrobe, Knitbone wondered what "ye other dead things" would be like. He hoped all their bits stayed together and they smelled nice. He hoped they wouldn't be mean, or be zombies or have a fondness for cats. He supposed that as *he* was dead and *they* were dead, they at least had something in common. Plus Floppy

Bernard never *once* laughed at his jokes.

A thrilling thought suddenly occurred to him. Maybe they could help him to make contact with the Peppers? *S.O.S.* sounded like a very grand and serious organization. They certainly sounded as if they knew what they were doing. Professional *and* spooky – oh yes, he liked the sound of that.

Finally, after a claw-biting wait, Tuesday teatime came and it was finally time to meet the members of S.O.S.

Knitbone knew that first impressions counted, so had done his best to flatten his fur into a presentable shape and licked his nose until it shone. This was no easy task because he kept sneezing and untidying himself in the process. He chewed some mint from the garden and rolled in a lavender bush for a finishing touch, which meant he had to start the fur-flattening process all over again. Finally, Knitbone Pepper looked and smelled, as Lord P would say, "absolutely smashing".

Arriving on time, Knitbone politely pawed at the barn door, pushing it open and casting a shaft of dusty yellow light through the open gap. He peered in. Cobwebs hung like grim bunting from the rafters. A spindly grey spider glared at him for a long moment and then scuttled into a gloomy corner.

There, sitting in a pool of late afternoon sunlight in the middle of the cool, stone floor, was a snowy goose and a nut-brown hare.

Knitbone looked around for their people. Who were these animals? Where were the *people* ghosts?

The goose spied him with piercingly bright blue eyes. "Ah, here he is – right on time!" he squawked, swooping over and whisking away the packet of ginger nuts.

Knitbone crossed the threshold and quietly sat down, tucking his tail meekly underneath him. This was not at all what he had expected; for a start, *they were animals*. When he'd been alive, all encounters with animals had been reliably short and generally ended with a high-speed chase. He hoped they didn't know that.

"Take a seat, young man – yes, over there, come-along-come-along! Welcome, welcome, *WELCOME* to S.O.S. – Spirits of Starcross. My name is Gabriel Pepper," honked the goose. "And this is Valentine Pepper…" He flapped his wings and gestured at the hare. "Is everybody here? Yes? Well, let's get on with it then." He ruffled his white feathers and made himself comfortable.

"Friends and comrades, today is a momentous day. It is a *special* day when we, at long last, welcome a new face to our little group of Pepper Beloveds." The hare bowed politely and the goose continued.

"Personally, I am *thrilled*, and I know you all are too. However I *must insist* that everyone remains calm, as he's probably very nervous."

You all? thought Knitbone, confused and looking about. *But there are only two of you. And what's a* Beloved?

Gabriel came very close to Knitbone's ear and shouted, "You don't have a clue what's going on, do you, dear? How does the saying go, Valentine?"

The brown hare called Valentine stood up on his long hind legs and, in a voice as smooth as melted fudge, announced, "*New recruits are easily spooked*," then sat back down again.

They both stared at Knitbone as if he were an interesting museum exhibit they longed to poke. This went on for an uncomfortably long time. Knitbone thought that now might be a good moment to introduce himself.

"Hello, Starcross, er…Spirits." He held out his paw. "Thank you for inviting me. I should

introduce myself. My name is Knitbone Pepper
and I think I am a ghost. An *animal* ghost,
that is."

They continued to stare at
him for a long second and
then exploded with
laughter. A tiny yellow
monkey, wearing a pearl
earring and a little
white ruff, dropped
at high speed
from the
rafters.

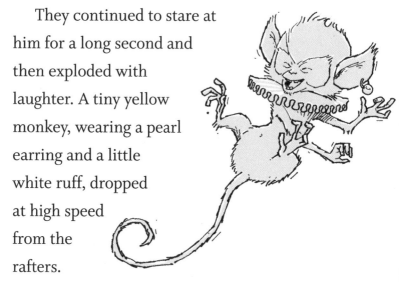

"We know 'oo you *are,* you silly woof-face,"
squeaked the monkey, doing a nippy backflip
into the centre of the group. "You are Winnie's
friend, ze one oo drinks from the magic well in
the wishy-washy room." He jumped up between
Knitbone's ears, stretched out the tiniest little
finger and jabbed Knitbone right in the eye.

"OW!"

The monkey roly-polyed down Knitbone's back and lay in a fit of giggles on the floor. "Oh, you funny, *funny* woof-face, you make-a me so 'appy I feel a leeetle bit sick in ma tummy. I shall love you always." He swung back up and planted a big smacker on the top of Knitbone's head. "We will be ze best friends for ever."

"My apologies, dearest Knitbone Pepper, and a thousand welcomes," purred Valentine, stroking his long ears. "This is Orlando Pepper. He is rather overexcited. You're quite, quite mad, aren't you, dear?"

Orlando nodded enthusiastically and promptly smacked himself hard on the head with a teaspoon.

Before Knitbone had had a chance to recover, a deep voice boomed from the shadows. "SO, KNITBONE PEPPER, YOU HAVE FINALLY CHOSEN TO BE WITH THE DEAD?"

Knitbone spun around in alarm. Another ghost? How many were there? This one sounded really scary. He was about to start begging for mercy when a podgy hamster wearing a scabbard and waving a sword strode out of the gloom.

"MARTIN," honked Gabriel, flapping his wings crossly. "*Really!* That was not very nice! You're not supposed to spook him, remember? You know he's only just coming out of Stage One – Denial. Say sorry at once."

"Yes, stop showing off, *Martin*!" tutted Valentine smugly.

Martin let out a high-pitched whine and stamped his little hamster foot. "Just 'cos you're the *oldest*, Valentine, it doesn't mean you can tell me what to do! Can he, Gabriel?"

The goose folded his wings firmly. "No squabbling, you two. Where are your manners?"

Martin huffed, kicked his sword sulkily and muttered, "Sorry, Knitbone. I was only having a bit of a laugh. I'm Martin Pepper. Welcome to S.O.S."

"What's Stage One Denial?" asked Knitbone.

"Oh, you know," said Martin. "The bit when you pretended you hadn't died after all."

"Oh," said Knitbone, a bit embarrassed. "You know about that?"

"Of course!" squealed Orlando happily, tickling Knitbone's ears. "Everyone craaaazy at the start. You were mad as buzzybee in bucket."

"So," continued Gabriel, "onwards and upwards." He took out a piece of paper headed *Very Important Matters for S.O.S.*

Knitbone's ears pricked up; this was more like it! S.O.S. sounded exciting – its very name suggested danger. So the Very Important Matters were most likely to do with good and evil. There might even be an opportunity for Knitbone to try out any new mysterious-and-as-yet-unknown ghost powers.

Knitbone tried to listen closely to what Gabriel was saying. This wasn't easy as Valentine, Martin and Orlando were all bickering over who should sit next to him, squashed up and elbowing each other out of the way.

"Now we come to Item Two on the agenda." Gabriel looked down at Knitbone with great solemnity. "I am sorry that we should have the misfortune to discuss something so serious at your first meeting, Knitbone Pepper, but these things need to be tackled head-on. Remember – it's all good experience."

Sandwiched between a hare and a hamster and with the monkey balanced on his nose, Knitbone nodded enthusiastically. Was it a bad ghost? Were the Peppers in trouble? Did they need his help? Because he really, *really* wanted to help. A low growl rumbled in his throat. Whatever it might be, he was ready for anything, and he was ready to fight to the death (in a manner of speaking).

Gabriel took a deep breath and announced with great seriousness, "Comrades, I'm very sorry to tell you...that the squeaky ironing board has finally been thrown away."

There was a collective groan of horror and a

clanking noise as Orlando
headbanged his spoon in
an act of despair.

"That's right,
dearhearts," continued
Gabriel, holding his wings aloft
in a dramatic gesture. "Despite our best efforts
– Valentine with his oil, Martin with his butter
and Orlando with his – well, we're not quite sure
what *that* was – nothing can be done."

A squeaky ironing board? What was going on?
This was not battling against forces of evil.
Knitbone had hoped there might be mention of
some sort of dashing uniform at least – something
involving flags and shields, perhaps.

As the meeting went on, it emerged that S.O.S.
weren't so much heroic defenders as domestic
caretakers of Starcross Hall. Their duties included
protecting the Peppers from things like out-of-date
muffins, or the top being left off the toothpaste.

Further Very Important Matters on the agenda included:

Item 3: The leak in the pantry ceiling.
Item 7: Lord Pepper's achy knee.
Item 15: Martin's heroic rescue of the
TV remote control from the bread bin.

Nibbling his ginger biscuit politely, Knitbone couldn't help feeling that these ghosts weren't spooky at all. He felt disappointed, but he didn't say so in case he appeared rude.

"Are you alright, Knitbone?" asked Martin, whipping out a tiny telescope from his utility belt and pointing it in his general direction.

56

"Only, you look like you've seen a ghost…
AHAHAHAHAHA!"

Knitbone suddenly and unexpectedly missed
his wardrobe.

"I think I've got a headache coming on," he
said, backing towards the barn door. "I really must
go and have a lie-down… Thank you very much
for having me, it's been very interesting, but I
have to go now…"

Gabriel put down the agenda and waddled over
to a calendar hanging on the barn wall. He blew
away the cobwebs and began to count off the days.
"Ah, yes… We can see here that Knitbone Pepper
has now reached Stage Two, otherwise known as
The Miserable Stage. Mustn't tire him out…
Same time next week!" squawked Gabriel after
Knitbone's retreating form. "Oh, and Knitbone."
The goose fixed him with a brilliant blue eye.
"Don't forget the biscuits."

Knitbone plodded back to the house,

pondering his new situation. The ghosts were as nutty as…ginger nuts. Just his luck to meet ghosts who were animal crackers. It was a peculiar sort of welcome, but you couldn't ignore that they were trying very hard to make him feel wanted. Plus, they all seemed to be called Pepper, which made him feel at home.

In fact, as he wandered across the courtyard, Knitbone was so engrossed in his own thoughts that he almost walked straight past the person hiding in the hedge.

Chapter 5
Hedge Hider

All sorts of things lived in hedges, Knitbone knew, but none of them – to his knowledge – *tutted*.

Intrigued, he nosed amongst the privet leaves and was shocked to discover a crotchety woman crouched in the middle of the shrubbery.

Straight away, Knitbone identified a Big Bark situation.

Knitbone was not shy when it came to intruders. He had been a very good guard dog when he had been alive, although he had tended to bark at most things, whether they were dangerous or not. This included squirrels, bees and, inexplicably, suitcases.

Hackles up, tail straight as a flagpole, he woofed very loudly in the woman's ear. Normally, the sight of a shaggy mutt, drooling and howling, was enough to make anyone back away. In fact, Knitbone's personal perfume (*damp rug with notes of salami*) had often been all it took to send people running for the hills. As it was, the lady didn't seem to notice at all. Unbothered, she stayed put, hunched up like a grumpy hedgehog, squinting through her little oval glasses, writing in a red notebook. Disappointed and defeated, Knitbone peered over her arm.

The notebook seemed to be full of scribbles. On closer inspection of the page, he could see that she had drawn a picture of the house with a list of sums at the side. Knitbone growled.

He sniffed at the hedge hider; she smelled just
like the dusty, unpaid electricity bills on the
kitchen window sill. She smelled of bother.

Just at that moment, the enormous front door
to Starcross Hall creaked wearily open. Lord
Pepper strolled into the weed-speckled courtyard,
yawned and gave a big stretch. The hedge stranger
stopped scribbling immediately, holding both her

breath and her pencil very, very still. Knitbone leaped out of the shrubbery and bounded around frantically. "Lord Pepper, there's a lady – and I think she might be *a bad lady* – right here!" He pointed with his nose. "Hiding just there in the hedge! Never fear, Knitbone's here!"

But of course, Lord Pepper could not heed Knitbone's warning, having no idea that Knitbone was there at all. Instead he looked up at the suddenly darkening sky, pulled his tattered admiral's hat down around his ears and went back inside to the warmth of the kitchen fire. It looked as if a storm was coming.

Chapter 6

Ghoul School

A week passed and Knitbone felt a bit better. He had been worrying about the hedge hider, but it wasn't as if he could do anything about her. Instead he soothed himself with the notion that it might even have been a dream. Everything was a bit strange these days.

His mind was on other things too, not least the fact that it was time for the next S.O.S. meeting. He knew this because a reminder card had been pushed under the wardrobe door.

Biscuit duty
Woof-Face ☺

It was always nice to be relied on for something, thought Knitbone as he "borrowed" yet another packet of ginger nuts from the pantry. He liked having responsibility. It was in his bones to be a faithful friend, and when somebody asked him to "fetch", well, it was too much to resist. They weren't such a bad lot. Besides, he had some important questions that needed answering.

When Tuesday teatime arrived, Knitbone let himself into the barn, sat down in the circle and rolled the pack of ginger nuts into the middle of the stone floor. The assembled group fell upon the biscuits, and in a matter of seconds there was nothing left but a small pile of crumbs and an empty packet.

A grey spider dropped from the roof and landed – *plop* – on the cobblestone floor.

Looking shiftily about, her eight eyes glittering like pewter sequins, she grabbed a fangful of crumbs. Then she scuttled back into the shadows, muttering darkly about "greedy-ghosty-guts".

"She puts the creepy in crawly, that one does," whispered Martin. Knitbone was about to ask if she was a Beloved too when Gabriel, wiping the corners of his beak with a small lace hanky, stepped on to a hay bale and began his speech.

"As you know, dearhearts, I am responsible for choosing books for our monthly book club. This week I discovered a real treasure in the library, something to get properly stuck into. It's the one we've all been waiting for…*The Big Book of Manure!*"

Knitbone raised a paw. He was feeling much braver this time. "Actually, Gabriel, I know I'm new here, but do you mind if we talk about something else first?"

"Oh, heavens above, yes, please!" said Valentine, rolling his eyes to the skies and fanning himself with a large leaf. Gabriel sat down in a huff.

"I've got an important question," began Knitbone hesitantly. "If you don't mind me asking, what is the point of all *this*?" He gestured to the group.

Martin the hamster leaped up and thrust his little pink hand in the air.

"OOOH! OOOH! I know the answer to this one. Gabriel's the librarian goose; he likes to talk about books. And our job is to sit here and stay awake."

"*No.*" Knitbone shook his ears. "What I mean is, what's the *point*? It's just that I'm a bit confused. Am I right in thinking that we are supposed to be proper ghosts? Shouldn't we be doing something a bit spookier and more important than eating biscuits and worrying about ironing boards? For example, I was hoping to get in touch with Winnie."

The group looked at each other in surprise. There was a bit of an awkward silence. This was fighting talk. Eventually Gabriel spoke up. "Well now, young Knitbone," he gabbled, rather defensively. "Beloveds consider haunting to be most impolite, not to mention that we are much-much-much too busy."

Knitbone raised a quizzical eyebrow. "Hmm. Busy doing *what* exactly?"

"Er…well, we're *guardians*; we look after things. Things such as important books." Gabriel looked round for support.

Valentine washed his whiskers and stroked his ears. "It's not easy being this handsome, you know."

Knitbone fixed his eyes on Martin, who just looked blank and shrugged. "Me? Dunno. I just hang about eating stuff."

The monkey was missing. "Where's Orlando?"

"He's probably out stealing spoons," explained Martin. "He loves shiny spoons. Little monkey can't get enough of 'em."

"*Spoons?* Is that the best a ghost can come up with? What about how I'm going to get back in touch with Winnie?" Knitbone felt suddenly annoyed. These ghosts weren't really how he had thought at all. Their ghostly edge was about as sharp as a feather duster. "Your invitation clearly said 'yours spookily'," he said crossly. "Dogs need something proper to *do*."

"You'll get used to it," protested Gabriel.

"I don't WANT to get used to it!"

"But you *will* get used to it."

"Uh-oh," said Valentine, getting up and checking the calendar. "Stage One – Denial. Yes… Stage Two – Miserable. Yes… Brace yourselves, boys! Here comes Stage Three, otherwise known as The Rage Stage. Watch out, everybody…"

"GRRRRRR!" Knitbone grabbed *The Big Book of Manure* with his teeth and hurled it into a dusty corner.

"Steady on, chap, I know it's a pile of old poo being dead, but there's no call for that sort of thing," shouted Valentine. Gabriel's beak began to wobble.

"Yes, *bad* dog, Knitbone. In your bed!" shouted Martin, pointing to the corner.

This seemed to do the trick. Knitbone calmed down and put his paws over his nose. "Sorry. Really sorry. I'm not normally like this. I don't mean to be rude, it's just that I miss…"

Now it was Knitbone's turn to go wobbly, and his tail hung low between his legs. "I miss being alive; I don't *want* to be dead. I miss my Peppers, but, most of all, I really, really, *really* miss Winnie."

Martin patted Knitbone's paw. "Don't worry, old chap, it's normal to be sad. *I* used to have a special Pepper too, you know. We all did," he whispered, as the group gazed at him sympathetically. "A Beloved is the most loyal sort of ghost. We stick around, just in case we might be needed again; you never know. All that devotion doesn't just disappear because of a silly thing like death. But it gets easier with time."

Valentine sighed. "We know what it's like, but we don't want to scare anybody, do we? A ghost pet isn't everybody's cup of tea. Don't worry, you're not on your own now."

THE BIG BOOK OF MANURE

With this
the barn door
burst open,
and Orlando
stood
triumphant,
silhouetted
against the golden
evening light, waving his shiny swag:
"I 'AVE ZE SPOONS!"

Over the next few days, Knitbone tried to put his
worries to one side and instead spent some time
learning about his fellow spooks.

Valentine the hare was the oldest resident
of Starcross Hall; he'd been there for 823 years.
A medieval knight's mascot, he'd met his end in a
jousting tournament. Perched in his master's lap,
the brown hare had died a noble death. Next
came Elizabethan Orlando, who fell down a well

showing off. Gabriel, a Cavalier goose, was killed trying to defend the Starcross library from the Roundhead army over 350 years ago. Martin had fallen victim to a dodgy Scotch egg at the Second World War VE Day celebrations in 1945.

The gang of Beloveds liked to go outside to the little Starcross chapel graveyard, sit on their people's tombstones, swing their legs, nibble biscuits and remember the past. Sometimes they would water the plants or do a little light weeding. Together, they had watched over Starcross and the Peppers for nearly a thousand years, trying to make themselves useful. They were the self-proclaimed official Guardians of the Estate. Although this sounds remarkable, the job was rarely glamorous or exciting, as Starcross was a very peaceful place. S.O.S. had been set up by Gabriel to help pass the time. The Beloveds had given Knitbone a useful handout:

Handy Hints and Tips for the New Beloved

1. **Beloveds:** A Beloved's love for their special human is so strong that they do not fade away. They are the most loyal and brave of all animal ghosts and will defend their people and their home to the last.

2. **Home Sweet Home:** Home is where a Beloved's heart is. Crammed full of happy memories of the past and their person, it is the only place for them. Attached in more ways than one, a Beloved is tied to their home for ever.

3. **Biscuits:** Ghosts eat ginger biscuits for energy – no other biscuit makes a ghost feel more alive. Chocolate ones make them sleepy. Pink wafers make them extremely naughty.

4. **Moving Things:** Small things can be moved (i.e. books, biscuits, etc.,) without drawing attention. It's amazing what non-believers

don't see, even when it's right under their noses. Being spotted requires a lot of extra OOMPH. Haunting is an advanced skill.

5. Haunting: Human ghosts are famous show-offs, always going on about themselves and being terrifying. Beloveds have smaller egos and nicer manners. They are careful NOT to scare their person. Haunting is considered rude and happens only in emergencies.

6. What to Wear: Ghosts are normally invisible to the Living. Any outfits slip into the ghost realm too, so a funny hat won't be noticed. This is fortunate because Beloveds are very fond of fancy dress. The idea of ghosts in sheets is nonsense made up by writers – Beloveds wouldn't be seen dead in one.

7. Friendship: Most animal ghosts are very friendly and like to help. Beware of Bad Eggs.

8. Keeping Busy: If you are a ghost, you are here for ever, so get used to it. Even better, get a hobby.

After a bumpy start, Knitbone had actually begun to cheer up and settle into a routine with his new ghost family. He was really beginning to find his paws.

The other members of S.O.S. had also become very fond of their new recruit and wanted to do what they could to help. Whenever he was down, the others reminded Knitbone that Winnie might notice something one day, so to keep his chin up. Martin suggested it might help if they mingled more with the Peppers in the daytime, and they all agreed. Knitbone was very touched by this gesture, especially as they all seemed rather awkward and self-conscious. They were clearly out of practice and felt a bit shy.

They began by hanging around in the garden, watching Lady P digging the vegetable patch and Lord P tending his bees. Occasionally, they muttered advice about slugs and greenfly, but it fell on deaf ears.

Every so often, Knitbone thought he caught
sight of the spindly grey spider he'd seen in the
barn, watching them from the sidelines. He didn't
know why exactly, but she made his fur creep.
The others explained that this was Mrs Jones.

"She's not a Beloved," whispered Valentine
out of the corner of his mouth. "She's a Bad Egg."

Knitbone opened his mouth to say more but
Valentine interrupted him. "Don't ask. Just stay
out of her way and, if you're lucky, she'll stay
out of yours."

When they got braver, the ghostly pals were to be found in the family bathroom, covering their

eyes and pushing the shampoo within grasping distance of soapy fingers.

Sometimes they slept at the end of Winnie's bed, piled up in a big ghostly heap.

THE FATAL BLOW

It didn't take long before they were putting on theatrical extravaganzas in the huge kitchen whilst the Peppers ate their dinner.

They hoped that their efforts would pay off and, one day, somebody would notice something. Although, being invisible, that wasn't likely.

In the meantime, everybody was having fun and Knitbone felt something close to happiness. It wasn't as exciting as being alive, but he did like being in a gang, taking up new interests and enjoying biscuits responsibly. Even the wardrobe was taking on a homely feel.

At least he could see Winnie every day too, even if she couldn't see him. A month had passed and he missed her terribly, but Knitbone was prepared to wait as long as it took, bumbling along in her shadow. Life for the Peppers – both dead and alive – went on.

Chapter 7

A Serious Business

Knitbone liked to check the post every morning. Mostly it was leaflets for pizza restaurants or double glazing offers. Today however, a brown envelope arrived. It was addressed to Lord Hector Pepper. Marked URGENT AND CONFIDENTIAL, Knitbone gave it a good sniff and promptly sneezed in disgust: more boring, dusty bother.

He left it on the doormat, blissfully unaware that it contained a ticking paper time bomb, poised to blow the Peppers' way of life to smithereens...

Knitbone was nosing amongst the music books in the ballroom, trying to settle on a hobby. He was looking for a copy of *Easy Piano Tunes for Beginners* when the door burst open and Winnie flew in. She was clutching the brown envelope in one hand and a letter in the other. Knitbone sat on the piano stool and watched as Winnie thrust the letter anxiously at her father, who was snoozing in a battered armchair.

Lord Pepper took the letter, put his reading glasses on, inspected it and nodded seriously. He patted Winnie's hand and said in a soothing tone, "Don't worry, Winnie. Stuff and nonsense, nothing to fret about, you'll see. It's all under control."

As Winnie's footsteps faded away up the corridor, Knitbone watched Lord Pepper read the letter again. Then, quite certain his daughter had gone, he screwed the letter up, tossed it behind the armchair and settled back down to sleep.

Knitbone jumped down from his stool and trotted over to have a look at the letter. Luckily his reading was coming on a treat since Gabriel had made him a reading star chart. He had recently moved on from picture books to chapter books (although he secretly missed the pictures). Knitbone flattened out the letter on the wooden floorboards and carefully sounded out the words…

BARTONSHIRE COUNCIL – URGENT

April 21st

Dear Lord Pepper,

It has come to my attention that the Pepper family estate owes
Bartonshire Town Council a SPECTACULARLY large sum
of money.

According to our records, in 1720, Montague Pepper (10th Lord of
Starcross Hall) borrowed twelve pennies from Bartonshire Local
Treasury in order to purchase a machine to "Extract ye sunbeams
from cucumbers". Over the centuries the debt has grown.
You now owe us: ONE MILLION POUNDS.

We would like our money back NOW please, thank you very much.
However, if you do not have a million pounds (which you obviously
don't), then you leave me no choice. If you do not pay up within
three days, then Starcross Hall, its land and contents, will be seized
and sold at a Council auction on May 25th.

Yours menacingly,
Mrs Nora Sockpuppet H.O.B.T.C.
(Head of Bartonshire Town Council)

P.S. I hear it's a horrible damp old dump – even your hedges
smell peculiar.

"*WHAAAT?*" Knitbone stared wide-eyed at the letter. There had to be some sort of misunderstanding. He read it again and again, trying to make sense of it.

Who did this Nora Sockpuppet think she was? Starcross wasn't just any old house, it was their *special home*! It couldn't be sold to a stranger – the idea was ridiculous. The Peppers *couldn't* be parted from the place…or could they? An ember of doubt began to flicker in Knitbone's heart. With a horrible sinking feeling, he remembered Number 2 on the *Handy Hints and Tips* handout.

2. A Beloved is tied to their home for ever.

Tied? OH NO! He did a panicky sum in his head.

$$(Starcross + Knitbone\ Pepper) - Winnie\ Pepper = Misery\ For\ Ever$$

What if Winnie was forced to leave Starcross and he was left behind? He'd be stuck here and she'd be gone! He couldn't bear to be separated from Winnie for ever. Being dead was bad enough, but losing Winnie completely was just too awful to imagine. Things were going from bad to worse. He read the letter again, trying to make sense of it, until a sentence jumped out at him: *Even your hedges smell peculiar.*

The memory popped up like a toadstool. Of course – the lady in the hedge! Had the hedge hider been from the council? He bounded around to the front of the chair. This was definitely another Big Bark situation.

"LORD PEPPER, CAN YOU HEAR ME?" Knitbone woofed. "Wake up and listen! This is very serious! YOU MUST DO SOMETHING!"

But Lord Pepper, who was very good at ignoring the unpleasant things in life, was already dreaming again, and didn't even flinch. Knitbone tried to pant slowly and think calmly.

Why was that Sockpuppet woman *hiding* in the hedge? Why go to all the trouble of digging up a debt that was nearly 300 years old? Why hadn't anybody ever mentioned this debt before? He growled to himself suspiciously as thoughts pinged around his brain like a ball bearing in a pinball machine.

There was only one thing for it. He grabbed a packet of ginger nuts from the pantry, marched straight over to the barn and called an emergency S.O.S. meeting.

Chapter 8
Woof-face Worries

"If everyone has quite finished bickering about the number of biscuits, I believe Knitbone has something to say."

"Yes, thank you, Gabriel, I certainly do. Orlando, can you take notes, please?" The little monkey picked up a piece of chalk, licked it with his tiny tongue and proceeded to write WOOF-FACE WORRIES on the barn wall.

"Er, thank you. It has come to my attention that Starcross is in Big Trouble. As you know,

Lord and Lady P are the best sort of people in the world, but I suspect their brain watches are set to daft o'clock." (It was true. Once Lord Pepper had a pigeon living in his dressing gown for a month and he didn't even notice.)

Martin clutched at his chubby cheeks. "Oh no! Not the badgers in the ballroom again?"

"No. I'm afraid to say that it's even worse than that." Knitbone cleared his throat and read out the letter.

Everyone began to talk at once.

"Ridiculous. There have always been Peppers at Starcross Hall. That 'cucumber sunbeam' stuff sounds made up," said Martin.

"Zees eez *disgrace*," muttered Orlando.

"Hmmm," said Valentine thoughtfully, twiddling his long ears and inspecting the letter. "Well, it *might* be genuine. Monty Pepper *was* a terrible experimenter. Blew up the observatory once… His wife Arabella was so cross she took away his favourite telescope and he sulked for a month. Extracting sunbeams from cucumbers sounds just like him."

"What a nerve. How does this Sockpuppet person know that Starcross is 'a horrible damp old dump' anyway?" Gabriel looked most offended. "Nobody from the council has ever so much as visited. In fact, *nobody* ever visits."

"Oh yes, we'd definitely have known," said Martin. "That sort of thing doesn't go unnoticed by S.O.S., no sir-eeee. Nothing gets past us." The hamster puffed out his chest proudly, before crinkling his nose and sniffing the air. "By the way, can anyone else smell that?"

It is a little known fact that ghost blushes smell of peppermint. Everyone looked at Knitbone, who in turn looked embarrassed and stared very hard at the floor.

"Well," he confessed, "I saw a strange lady hiding in the hedge three weeks ago, but I couldn't scare her away – even though I tried to – so…I didn't tell anyone. I knew she was up to no good. It turns out that SHE was the council visitor." He looked up guiltily. "I'm really sorry."

"Don't worry," said Valentine. "You weren't to know."

"It's all my fault." Knitbone put his paws over his ears miserably. "I knew she was up to something and I should have done something really *scary*."

Valentine smiled. "We're only ghosts, you ninny, we're not real. Well, not *really* real, anyway."

Martin sighed despairingly. "Knitbone, we don't actually DO serious stuff. I thought you'd have noticed that by now."

Knitbone's ears and tail drooped. "But this is an emergency! I thought that in an emergency things might be, you know…different."

"Don't feel too-too-too bad, Knitbone," said Gabriel, putting a wing around Knitbone's shoulders. "Anyway," the goose continued in a soothing tone, "it'll be perfectly alright. Nothing bad ever happens here. There will be Peppers at Starcross for ever – always have been, always will be. Nothing will come of it, you'll see."

It was true that if the Peppers were known for anything, then it was their staying power; they clung to Starcross Hall like barnacles. Everyone agreed that this was probably just a storm in a

teacup. Everyone, that is, except Knitbone.
Something bad was around the corner.
He could smell it.

Three days later, Nora Sockpuppet,
Head of Bartonshire Town Council, arrived
at Starcross Hall. She hammered on the front
door and gleefully delivered a court order into
Lord Pepper's shocked hand. It gave them two
choices – pay up immediately or sell. In truth,
it wasn't a choice at all. They didn't have one
million pounds, so Starcross had to be sold
to pay the debt and there was absolutely
nothing they could do about it.

Grinning like a tiger, Nora marched
back down the path to the rusty front
gates and screwed a sign firmly
onto one of them.

The spooks stood in front of the iron gates, beak and jaws dropped, staring up at the sign in horror.

NO. This was *impossible*, completely *impossible*. Starcross Hall couldn't be sold! It was unthinkable; it had been their home for centuries. They belonged to Starcross and Starcross should belong to the Peppers, not to anyone else.

"Oh no, no, NO! This is very, very bad," fretted Martin.

"Told you, didn't I?" whined Knitbone, tail tucked between his legs. "Didn't I say so? *'It's just a storm in a teacup, Knitbone'.*" Knitbone's ears drooped. "What about me and Winnie?" he whimpered. "What if we run out of time and she never finds out that I'm still here? Oh-oh-oh-noooooooooooooooOOOOO!" Knitbone began to howl at the sky inconsolably.

"*Shush*, Knitbone!" Gabriel stomped around in a circle, stretching his white wings out wide, flapping and squawking. "Listen here, nobody-nobody-NOBODY is going to buy Starcross!" The goose was almost glowing with rage (it was actually rather impressive) and Knitbone was suddenly reminded of Gabriel's heroic past as the Starcross library's saviour.

"Starcross Hall belongs to the *Peppers* and to *us*. No more Mister Nice Goose." Gabriel's blue eyes narrowed and took on a look of steely determination. "S.O.S. – this is the biggest crisis to face us in our 904-year history. This is an emergency and it's time to rise to the challenge. Beloveds, follow me. Strangers are moving into Starcross over our dead bodies."

Chapter 9

Fighting Fit

G abriel marched into the house, and swept along the corridor to the library, the rest of the spooks trailing despondently behind him. He headed straight for the ladder leaning against the shelves, and after a bit of a struggle (and some undignified heaving on Knitbone's part), the goose teetered on the top rung, running his beak along the spines.

"What are you doing, Gabriel?" asked Knitbone.

"Let me see, I'm sure it's here somewhere… *Alchemy for Beginners… The Poems of… A Guide To…* Ah, here we are."

He selected a dusty old book, pulled it out with his beak, and tipped it off the edge of the shelf. The book plummeted to the floor and landed with a heavy thud on the dusty carpet. Everyone gathered round. Bound in reddish-brown leather, it had a gold imprint of a plant on the front. It looked like a very old book indeed.

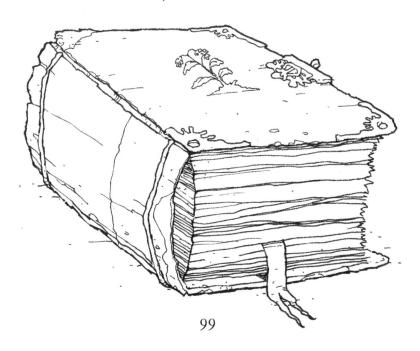

"*READING?* Now? *Really?*" Knitbone howled in frustration, and put his paws over his eyes. "How is *reading* going to help? You said it was an *emergency*!"

"It is! Knowledge is power, Knitbone," said Gabriel gravely.

Martin poked it suspiciously with his sword. "What's this then? Is it a special book?"

"It's not *just* a special book, Biscuit Brain," whispered Valentine with great reverence and awe. "It's THE special book."

Orlando clung to Gabriel's neck, his shiny eyes round like buttons. "Even more special than *Ze Big Book of Manure*?"

"Oh yes! Much more special than *The Big Book of Manure*," Gabriel replied. "The Handy Hints and Tips handout, The Three Stages – this is where they all come from. It's The Book; a manual containing highly-advanced, five-star, ghostly information." The goose opened the book to the first page and read out the title page. "*The Good Ghost Guide.*"

He tapped the page with a wing tip and fixed the others with a canny look. "Right, here's the plan. We are going to make Starcross *SO* terrifying, *SO* scary and *SO* downright spooky, that nobody in their right mind will bid on it at auction."

Knitbone's ears pricked up. "Proper, impolite, naughty, scary ghosts? Pawsome! About time too!" His tail wagged excitedly. He made a little growly sound to give an indication of how frightening he could be.

"Eez what ghosts are supposed to do best," Orlando nodded wisely, polishing a teaspoon with his tail.

"However," continued Gabriel, "I must confess that we are a *tiny bit* out of practice. We need to brush up on our ghostly skills. What we need is a refresher course." He turned the pages and read the opening words to Chapter 4.

"EXERCISE AND ATTACK: If disaster strikes, a ghost must be fighting fit and ready for battle. Top-notch haunting calls for top-notch fitness. Remember, an unfit ghost is unfit for purpose, like a chocolate saucepan or a jelly spade. A flabby phantom is a foolish phantom."

Martin glanced sideways to check no one was looking and sucked his tummy in.

Gabriel went on: "Tickling, prodding, poking, whispering, stinking and biting are all possible for the Healthy Haunter. With the right levels of fitness (and a loudspeaker) a ghost can even bellow like a buffalo! Ghosts may be invisible to the Living (NB: for rare exceptions see pg 84 on REUNITING) but a fighting spirit is a force to be reckoned with. Invisibility is an ability – use it wisely."

Knitbone's heart gave a giant leap and his tail wagged with hope. "Hang on…'exceptions'? What's reuniting? Hurry up! Turn to page 84!"

Gabriel sighed. He already knew the answer,

having asked that question himself many years ago. He turned to the place where page 84 should have been, but there was nothing there but a ragged edge of paper.

"It's been torn out!" whined Knitbone, his tail drooping. "Where's it gone?"

"I don't know, old boy," said Gabriel quietly, shrugging his wings. "It's just one of those things. Don't take it too hard."

Just my luck, thought Knitbone, trying hard to be brave, as the rest of the Beloveds leafed through the book.

It had lots of diagrams of PE lessons, and snippets of advice including worrying warnings about not eating too many biscuits. Clearly, if they were going to save Starcross, the ghosts needed to get in scary shape. The clock was ticking – fast. Training would begin that afternoon.

As the ballroom clock struck two, the Beloveds gathered in the courtyard at the front of the house and, after a lengthy period of stretching, groaning and yawning, they were ready to begin.

They started with the best of intentions. "It says here to begin with star jumps – sixteen precisely," woofed Knitbone, scanning down the page. "And then we can sprint to the bridge and back."

Once the star-jump spectacle was over, Valentine, Martin, Orlando and Gabriel jogged over to the curly iron gates and waited for Knitbone's whistle. "On your marks, get set, GO!"

They lumbered forwards, huffing, waddling, lolloping and trotting up the lane, cutting across the grassy fields and past the lake. They started well, but it wasn't long before they were out of puff, clutching at their chests and feeding each other emergency ginger biscuits.

"I really don't understand this," gasped Valentine, leaning on the bridge wall. "I've always been an excellent runner. I think I must be having an off day."

"An off century, more like," panted Martin, clutching at the stitch in his side.

"Come *on*, everyone, focus!" called Knitbone, who had trotted up behind them, shaking his head at the stopwatch. "And YOU!" – Orlando was dragging one of Lady Pepper's old handbags, bumping it along the ground – "I told you to leave the spoons at home!" Knitbone gave an exhausted sigh and slumped onto the ground. "This is hopeless. We are all way out of condition. We're never going to be ready in time. Is it any wonder we're about as spooky as spatulas?"

Valentine placed his hot head on the cool stone of the bridge and closed his eyes. "I'll be right as rain in five minutes," he gasped.

Gabriel lay on his back, wheezing asthmatically. "I think I'm dying again," he groaned, wings outstretched, feet pointing straight up at the sky.

"Look, I think somebody else should be in charge," Knitbone insisted. "I'm only a beginner, remember! I've only just learned about the danger of pink wafers. I don't think I can do this. This is a PE whistle, not a magic wand!"

Disheartened, they trooped back to the Starcross library, collapsing down on the threadbare carpet. The atmosphere was a bit tense. Valentine took out a new packet of ginger nuts hidden behind a book to share as a peace offering.

Whilst everyone was munching away, Valentine examined the gold illustration of a plant on the front cover of *The Good Ghost Guide*.

"I know that plant," he said suddenly. "It's called comfrey. It's on the Pepper Coat of Arms." He cocked a big ear towards the crest above the fireplace. There it was; a large floppy plant surrounded by crossed swords.

"No, it's not, it's called *wallwort*. It's in the garden," said Martin, proudly.

"No, eez called *ass ear*, you fool," said Orlando, as he threw a biscuit at the hamster.

Valentine tutted. "Calm down and stop bickering. Goodness, it's only a plant. Let's look it up, shall we?" He pulled down an encyclopaedia from a low shelf and flicked through it until he came across a picture of the plant. He cleared his throat and read out what it said underneath:

"*Officially known as comfrey (also known as ass ear, black root and wallwort), this useful plant is known for its magical healing properties, solving nearly all problems including pains, bruises and broken hearts. Witches, wizards, alchemists and herbalists refer to it as…*" Valentine stopped and stared at the page, golden eyes like saucers.

"What? What do they call it?" Martin squeaked.

Valentine took a deep breath and continued. "*Witches, wizards, alchemists and herbalists refer to it as <u>knitbone</u>.*" Valentine slammed the book shut in triumph. A strong smell of peppermint filled the room.

Orlando narrowed his eyes at Knitbone and jabbed him in the chest with a bony little finger. "First on crest, now on special book. YOU definitely in charge, Woof-face."

They made a gym in the attic above Winnie's bedroom, where the servants used to live, long, long ago. It had been abandoned for years, so it was nice and private. Also there were a few useful bits and bobs lying about here and there. It was the perfect place to get serious about sport.

Knitbone tried very hard and drew up personal fitness plans for them all.

They lifted weights: a mini-hairbrush for Orlando and a toothbrush for Martin. Gabriel even learned to do the splits. They danced, they skipped and they stretched. They ran on the spot and touched their toes. Valentine fashioned himself a knitted leotard out of an old hot water bottle cover and performed graceful cartwheels, handsprings and backflips across the attic.

After a week of hard work, the Beloveds were definitely starting to feel less wispy and more substantial.

"You know, it's strange, but ever since Knitbone arrived, I feel young again," giggled Valentine. "Young for 823, anyway!"

Knitbone timed Martin's laps as he scampered and puffed around the inside rim of an old bicycle wheel. "Fifty-five, fifty-six, fifty-seven… COME ON, MARTIN, YOU CAN DO IT!"

Gabriel chuckled, stretching his wings with a flap. "Me too. Seems like *this* old dog can teach us new tricks after all!"

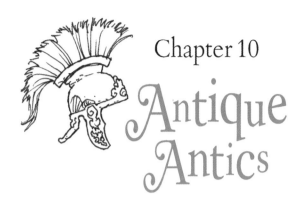

Chapter 10

Antique Antics

On Sunday, they decided to have a well-deserved evening off. Everyone had settled down to watch the TV in the big, cosy sitting room; the Peppers on the squashy sofa and S.O.S. on the big rug. A show about antiques was on, and they watched it every week. This was the Beloveds' favourite programme by far and they liked to think they knew better than the experts.

In this particular episode, a young woman had brought in a picture of a yellow wheatfield. It was in a gold frame and was very old. The expert went a funny colour and mopped his forehead with a spotty hanky. When he'd managed to calm himself down, he said it was by the famous painter, Vincent Van Fluff, and that it was worth a fortune.

"I know that painter!" spluttered Gabriel through a mouthful of ginger nut, spraying a blizzard of crumbs everywhere and pointing at the television. "Vinnie wotsit! He came on holiday and stayed with Cook – do you remember, Valentine? Such a nice young man. Mad as a box of frogs, though, always gawping at the stars and the flowers, taking his easel out into the fields, ginger hair sticking up all over the place."

S.O.S. had been so engrossed in the programme that they hadn't really noticed Lord Pepper desperately trying to explain the sale of Starcross once more to Winnie. In fact, they didn't really pay any attention *at all* until the shouting and crying started. It would be fair to say that Winnie was not taking the whole thing well…

"I will *never* understand! You *said* it was all under control!" yelled Winnie, balling up her fists, jumping up from the sofa and stamping her foot in frustration. "First Knitbone dies, and now THIS! Peppers have been at Starcross for hundreds of years. What would our ancestors say? How can you let this happen? For goodness' sake, take that silly hat off, Daddy! This is serious! You're supposed to be a grown-up – why are you just giving in?"

Lady Pepper put down her juggling clubs, placed her hand on Winnie's shoulder and sighed deeply. "Winnie, we are as poor as church mice. We love Starcross with all our hearts, but we don't even have a hundred pounds, never mind a million pounds!"

"We *have* tried Winnie, honestly," insisted Lord Pepper. "I caught the bus down to the council offices and offered them 247 jars of my yummy honey. Your mother offered the council a whole barrow of her mega-monster marrows, but they weren't interested." He lowered his voice to an embarrassed whisper. "Winnie, we even offered them our favourite hats, but they said no." He sniffed. "They just laughed at us, didn't they, Isadora?"

Lady Pepper nodded and wiped away a tear. "They did, Hector, they did. The truth is, we don't have anything worth that kind of money. All our things are so old, you see."

"Try to look on the bright side, Winnie," said Lord Pepper miserably. "Perhaps we can live in a caravan, drive off and see the world…"

"NO! I don't WANT to look on the bright side or live in a caravan! I won't leave. I won't. You *can't* make me." Winnie was furious. "This is *my* home! *I* belong here! I'm Starcross home-grown, remember?" She stared fiercely at her father. "Daddy, *Knitbone's* buried here!"

Winnie dashed upstairs to her bedroom and threw herself face down on the bed, closely followed by the Beloveds.

"It's not fair. Why did you have to go away?" she sobbed. She took out Knitbone's crumpled and tear-stained photograph from under her pillow. "I miss your nose. I miss your funny ears. I miss your twinkly eyes. If you were here now, you'd know what to do."

The ghosts surrounded Winnie's bed and watched her cry herself to sleep. Gabriel put a comforting wing around Knitbone's shoulder.

"She's a spirited little thing, isn't she?" said Valentine wistfully.

Knitbone's heart was in a whirl. The Peppers and Starcross needed their help now more than ever.

He put his nose close to Winnie's ear and whispered, "Don't worry, Winnie. You can still rely on me."

Later that evening, the Beloveds all gathered in the barn, to stock up on ginger biscuits and plan their battle strategy. After lots of discussion, Knitbone, large and in charge, stood up and raised his paws. With a dogged determination he began.

"Beloveds, the time has come. Tomorrow is Monday, and the first viewers are booked in to come and see Starcross. NOW is the time for ACTION! We must MOBILIZE! We are FIGHTING FIT and READY for WAR!" Everyone cheered like pirates, raising their biscuits. "We may not have any money to buy Starcross ourselves," Knitbone barked, "but we CAN make sure that nobody else buys it." He took a big bite out of a ginger nut and woofed, "S.O.S. TO THE RESCUE!"

Chapter 11

Team Spirit

Monday morning dawned bright and blue. Prospective buyers began traipsing up the lane, across the gravel courtyard and into Starcross Hall, tutting over the rusty suits of armour, inspecting the tatty oil paintings of long dead Peppers and running fingers along the dusty skirting boards.

They talked about what they could do to make the house more modern, or how their cats would like living there, taking out tape measures and humphing over the cracks in the walls.

Then, just as the conversation swung around to the subject of actually buying it, Orlando would unleash one of his spooky stinkers. It had an immediate and satisfying effect. Potential purchasers ran from the house, choking and clasping their hands to their faces, tears streaming down their cheeks.

S.O.S. had been studying the finer details of *The Good Ghost Guide* very closely. The book had a chapter called STONKING STINKS which told them everything they needed to know about creating off-putting smells. (It was also in the *Beginners* section, which was handy.)

These weren't just any old dodgy whiffs, but *really terrible, rotten reeks.* Imagine the worst smell EVER. Like cabbages and poo and pickled onions that had been made into an enormous smoothie. With fish sprinkles.

It was all a matter of focus really. Martin wasn't very good at it (he could only make the smell of buttered toast) but Orlando had a natural talent, concentrating so hard that his eyes bulged and his whole body trembled. What he produced was *astonishingly* awful.

For those people with colds or no sense of smell, the Beloveds had different plans. Always up for a bit of competition, they limbered up for the Trifle Splatting event. This involved "surprising" visitors by catapulting blobs of red and yellow mush at them, the aim of the game being to create the most chaos with the best-aimed splat. Extra points were awarded for speed, accuracy and style. To their great satisfaction Starcross soon resembled a pudding war zone. There was a good deal of blood-curdling screaming and, most importantly, *more people running away.*

And the Beloveds didn't stop there. Oh no.

They blew in people's ears and tickled their noses.

They rattled chains
and tied shoelaces together.

They threw plant pots and
pinched bottoms.

They knocked off
people's glasses and
filled their handbags
with freezing
cold water.

Best of all was when the visitors screeched
"NEVER!" or "This place is EVIL! You'd have to be
mad to buy it! AAAARRGGHHHHHHH!" and ran
screaming from the house.

S.O.S. were having the time of their deaths. They loved it when people screamed and howled. It was a hoot.

Completely unaware of the ghosts' battle plan, Winnie had her own ideas. Her parents might have given up, but she wasn't prepared to go down without a fight. She was determined to ruin all the viewings personally by putting buyers off, one by one.

Winnie made certain that all visitors were given a detailed explanation of the damp, and the blocked drains, and the dangerous electrics (which only occasionally worked as they had been chewed by rats). She told them that the roof had more holes in it than Swiss cheese, that savage wolves lurked in the woods near the bridge and that they had regular earthquakes. She told them all in no uncertain terms that they would be double bonkers to buy it.

Meanwhile, Lord Pepper had been spending

one half of his time talking to people about his hats. To his surprise, they often seemed a tired bunch, yawning a lot. The other half of his time had been spent making paper-thin excuses about the increasingly strange goings-on. Frankly, he preferred not to think about it. Lady P, who was a bit more practical, had opened the fridge and, after noticing that a trifle had inexplicably appeared with a catapult in it, had to admit that Starcross Hall was an odder place to live than ever, which was saying something.

Winnie, a down-to-earth sort of girl, thought that grown-ups had overactive imaginations. She'd lived at Starcross all her life and had never seen a single ghost. Ignoring the visitors' shrieks, she concluded there was always a logical explanation for everything, although she couldn't think what it might be just for the moment.

By the end of the week, news of the alleged

hauntings had spread like wildfire and viewers were beginning to cancel their visits left, right and centre. Spotting a sensational story, a journalist from the local paper arrived on the Peppers' doorstep. He asked them lots of excited questions, snapping away with his camera.

Lord and Lady Pepper tried to steer the conversation round to hats, bees and vegetables, but the journalist only wanted to know about the "ghostly activity". Lord P said innocently that he had no idea what the journalist was talking about and offered him another Jammy Dodger. S.O.S. followed the nervous reporter about, obligingly knocking things over and gleefully dropping plates with a crash.

A few days later, Lady Pepper was out buying seaweed crackers and pickles, when the front page of the local newspaper caught her eye:

BARTONSHIRE TIMES

SPOOKY STARCROSS SPIRITS HAUNT HORRIFIED HOMEBUYERS!

WHO WOULD BUY A HOUSE LIKE THIS?

Beneath the headline was a photograph of the Peppers standing next to the fireplace in the library, under their coat of arms. Lord Pepper was wearing his best crown, and Lady Pepper was looking confused in her rabbit pyjamas. Winnie just looked cross.

Lady P instantly dropped her shopping, grabbed a paper, flung a handful of coins and buttons on the counter and ran full pelt all the way home. She dashed through the open front door, skidded across the kitchen tiles and plonked the newspaper on the long wooden table, where Lord Pepper was about to crack open a nice boiled egg. He took one look at the front page, dropped his teaspoon with a clatter and whimpered in defeat. "Well, that's it then. NO ONE is going to want the old place now! Nora Sockpuppet will be furious. She'll think we've done this deliberately. What will the council do to us?" he wailed, his head in his hands. "Isadora, what are *we* going to *do*?"

S.O.S. sat on the table, reading the article. Thrilled, they high-fived each other and did a lot of WOO-HOOing. At last, all their hard work was paying off. Nobody wanted Starcross – hoorah and hoozah!

Winnie inspected the photo. They all looked terrible, so she was delighted. She could see the photographer had made it look as bad as possible, adding dark shadows here and there. It was even a bit blurry, to add extra spookiness. Right at the bottom of the picture, just by her feet was a particularly dark patch. She looked closer and to her surprise, noticed something peculiar. It looked a bit like the shape of a…

"*Winnie*," said Lady Pepper, throwing the newspaper into the recycling bin, "please go and fetch your father his fur-lined nightcap and a nice cup of beetroot tea. He's coming out in his nervous rash again."

Chapter 12

Beardy-Weirdy

"Hello, is that Hector Pepper, 18th Lord of Starcross Hall? Home of the infamous Starcross Spirits? Excellent. I hear your property is for sale. This is Krispin O'Mystery, Britain's Number One Ghost Hunter. I would like to make an appointment to come and view the house, please. I know…only three days left until the auction. I am looking for the right property. Yes, you heard me… That's right…as soon as possible… Tomorrow morning? First thing will be perfect. I may be with you for some time."

Krispin O'Mystery claimed he was the seventh son of a seventh son of a fortune-teller. He insisted that special supernatural skills flowed in his veins. He arrived in a bus, with an enormous airbrushed portrait on the side, declaring him to be a *Ghost Hunter Extraordinaire*.

He slid out of the front seat, sighed with self-satisfaction and strode across the courtyard. Krispin wore leather trousers that squeaked as he walked and he had a little pointy beard. His fingers were covered in crystal rings and his hair looked odd, like it had been knitted.

Krispin seemed to have brought a lot of noisy friends too, friends who spilled out of the bus like lentils from a leaky bag. They immediately set up camp in the orchard and someone began playing a nose flute.

Striding along in jangling cowboy boots, Krispin suddenly stood stock-still in the courtyard,

hand raised to the heavens and eyes closed, as if stunned by an invisible force.

"Ah, yes! There are many spirits here. Restless, desperate souls crying for their voices to be heard! Don't worry, Krispin O'Mystery will hear your woes!" His thrilled fans clapped.

Knitbone and the spooks looked down on the party from the attic window.

"We've got a right one here," grinned Martin. "This should be fun. He'll be gone faster than you can say 'beardy-weirdy'." He cracked his tiny hamster knuckles and did a bit of shadow boxing. "He's got no idea what he's letting himself in for."

Knitbone growled suspiciously. He wasn't so sure. A ghost hunter could be a problem; he wasn't likely to scare easily.

"Ah, Mr O'Mystery, welcome to Starcross Hall," said Lord Pepper, who had stood in the courtyard watching Krispin's arrival with interest. He stepped forward and cheerfully offered his hand. Krispin looked at it like it was a dead rat covered in porridge.

"I'm afraid I do not shake hands. It interferes with the Energy." Lord Pepper looked confused. "Now, if you will excuse me, I feel I am being drawn…" Krispin pressed his fingers to his temples "…to the library."

Krispin strode past Lord Pepper towards the open doorway, barking over his shoulder at a small rabbity-looking woman dressed in a tie-dyed blouse. "Meryl! Will you hurry up with the equipment?" Meryl squeezed through the crowd of admirers and staggered under the weight of a range of contraptions.

Krispin raced on ahead into the house.

Five minutes later, his voice streamed loudly through an open window in the library. "No, Meryl, I said *here*, not *there*! If I hadn't known you in a previous life, I honestly don't think I'd bother."

Meryl was setting up a complicated-looking machine with a number of different antennae, all pointing in different directions. 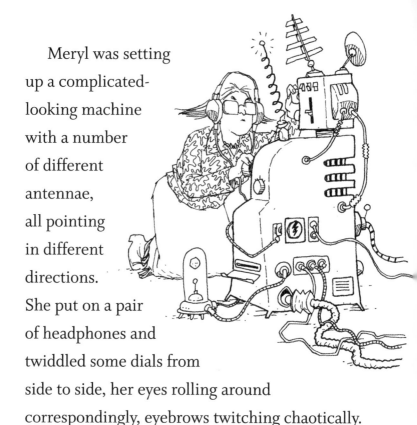 She put on a pair of headphones and twiddled some dials from side to side, her eyes rolling around correspondingly, eyebrows twitching chaotically.

Lord Pepper popped his head round the library door. "Mr O'Mystery, would you like me to show you about? I noticed you were very interested in that Chinese vase back there. A bit of guidance, perhaps? Only it is a bit…er…unusual here at the moment."

Krispin was admiring his reflection in a gilt-edged mirror, patting his hair. "You mean the famous Starcross Ghosts? They've put a lot of people off, haven't they? Not me, though." Krispin grinned a horrible sickly grin. "I *love* a live one. No, I have no need of your guidance, Lord Pepper. My guidance comes from the spirit realm…"

"Oh, I see." Lord Pepper didn't see.

"No, you just go about your business. You're not needed here."

"Oh, I see." (He still didn't see.) "Right then, I'll let you get on with…it." Lord Pepper wandered away, entirely unsure as to what "it" might be. He returned to the safety of his beehives, where everything made sense and all was right with the world.

By now the ghosts had trotted downstairs and padded into the library, where they sat listening closely to the ghost hunter.

"Well, it sounds like we're getting a bit of a name for ourselves, doesn't it?" noted Valentine, chewing on a blade of grass and sounding rather pleased. "Famous, eh? I *do* have unusually beautiful ears, though, now I come to think of it…"

"Don't be so vain, Valentine," said Martin. "Remember the Hints and Tips – human spooks get famous, not animal ghosts."

"Tell me about it. Look at headless horsemen," grumbled Valentine. "Nobody ever mentions the horse, do they? And to be fair, it's the horse doing all the work, isn't it?"

"But that's what makes us different to the human ghosts – remember?" said Knitbone absent-mindedly, wandering around the back of Meryl's machine. "Number 5 on the handout? We're here because we are Beloveds, not because we like showing off. It's about loyalty." He inspected the dials and the switches closely. "What's he up to? I wonder what this machine is actually supposed to *do*?"

Orlando clambered up the side of the fireplace onto the mantelpiece. From here he could comfortably reach the top of Krispin's head. He rummaged around in his hair for a bit and denounced it a
"nasty, woolly hat a bit like snoozy-cat".

"I think you mean a wig," chuckled Knitbone.

"Meryl, turn the Ghost-Locator-ator on," snapped Krispin, touching his hair, vaguely aware of something fiddling with it.

Obediently, Meryl flicked the switches, turned the dials up to full and adjusted her headphones. The machine began to hum like a swarm of bees, pulsing with coloured lights. A stream of paper spooled urgently out of the side, covered in data.

Krispin flung his arms out wide, took a deep breath and boomed, "Spirits of Starcross, hear my call! Is there anyone you would like to speak to on this mortal plane?"

S.O.S. looked at each other and shrugged. They'd never been on a plane. Knitbone had only been as far as the park.

Krispin tried again. "Do not be afraid, my friends, we are merely here to help you... OUCH!"

Martin, standing on the mantelpiece next to Orlando, and in easy reach of Krispin's flung-out hand, had bitten the end of his finger, very, very hard. Orlando clapped in rapturous delight.

"Oh, well done, Martin, excellent fitness and focus!" said Gabriel.

Meryl had her mouth open in a perfect "O" of surprise. Inspecting the end of his finger, Krispin noticed two little teeth marks. "Meryl," he whispered gravely. "This is serious stuff. Starcross is living up to its reputation. I think we might have a boggart. We must proceed with caution."

"What's a boggit?" asked Martin, affronted. "I'm not a boggit, I'm a hamster."

Valentine sighed in a world-weary manner. "Honestly, Martin, sometimes you are *so* unsophisticated and brash. A boggart is a naughty spirit. They were everywhere in my day. At least this man knows his stuff, unlike some creatures I could mention."

Knitbone and Gabriel looked at each other and raised their eyebrows.

"Well, he DOESN'T know his stuff, because I am NOT a poggit, I am a HAMSTER. And I *don't* have a rash." Martin was getting quite heated. "Whose side are you on anyway?"

Gabriel stood up. "Yes, Valentine, whose side are you on?"

"I'm just saying it's nice to be in the company of a professional, that's all." Valentine stretched his long legs and yawned. "Well, I've seen enough for now. I'm off to the attic. It's time for my exercises. See you later." He was gone in a flash.

Annoyed, Martin folded his arms, pouted and huffed. "Fine. Whatever. I'm going for a sleep then." With this he swung down from the fireplace and marched off in the opposite direction.

Knitbone sighed impatiently to himself. "So that leaves just me, Gabriel and Orlando. Brilliant."

"Hold on, hold on…Meryl, I've got something coming through…" Krispin was looking rather peculiar, all trembly and wobbly-eyed. "I have a spirit with me right now." The spooks looked around in surprise. They couldn't see anyone. Orlando even looked under the chair.

Krispin soldiered on in a spooky voice. "You are

coming through now, I can hear you… Your name is…*Olden Days Agatha*…and you are looking for your…er…bonnet…" Krispin was talking to thin air. He was clearly making it up.

Outraged by this blatant dishonesty, Orlando couldn't help himself. He jumped up into the air, did a backflip and rapped Krispin smartly on the forehead with a spoon.

"Naughty Krispy Fibbychops!"

"OUCH!"

Meryl rushed over to offer help, but Krispin brushed her away, grabbing the data sheets and inspecting the results greedily. "The Energies here are remarkable;

they are a tricky bunch indeed, and so easily provoked. Excellent. It's perfect." He smoothed his hair back and smiled. It wasn't a nice smile, like the sort you might give to a baby or the sort you might make whilst eating ice cream. It was a smile that stopped at Krispin's lips, never reaching his eyes.

"As you know, Meryl, I will not tolerate *difficult* ghosts. Not bad for a trial run, not bad at all." He looked up, wild-eyed and boomed, "We will return at midnight, when the spirits will be peaking." With this, Krispin and Meryl left the library and did their mysterious walk back up the corridor (which looked a bit like they'd been at the cooking sherry), retreating through the front door to their luxury bus.

"Well, I won't be peaking," Knitbone shouted after their departing backs. "My bedtime is nine o'clock. I'll be in my wardrobe, snoozing, like any sensible ghost who needs their beauty sleep!"

Chapter 13

Suck Up

"**K**NITBONE-KNITBONE-*KNITBONE*!"

There was a desperate hammering on the wardrobe door.

Knitbone swung the door open and squinted out at the moonlight. (Living in the middle of nowhere meant that Winnie rarely remembered to close her curtains.) He had an eye mask pushed up onto his forehead and looked very unhappy. "*What*, Martin," he growled, "could be so important that you have woken me up in the middle of the night?

I was having my best dream, the one where I am ALIVE doing ALIVE things. What do you want? Tell me quickly so you can go away again."

Martin swallowed hard to get past the lump in his throat and wrung his little hands urgently. Tears welled up in his eyes. "They've got Valentine. *Krispin's got Valentine.*"

"What the…? How? Calm down – what are you talking about?"

Martin gulped. "I was wide awake after my snooze, so I thought I'd go and have a biscuit or four to pass the time.

I was near the library at midnight when I heard Krispin's boring, droney voice going *on* and *on* so I thought I'd better have a peek... And Valentine was there, sat on one of the bookshelves! Meryl was fiddling with that machine-thing and Krispin went all wobbly-eyed again, saying stuff about how he could 'sense a wild creature of extraordinary speed and beauty' et cetera, et cetera, and...well...you *know* Valentine's a bit unusual like that, he's a sucker for a compliment... Anyway, next thing I know Krispin's opening a little glass box and then... and then..." Martin began to gulp and sob again.

"Martin! What is it?" Knitbone gave the hamster a little shake. "*What happened?*"

Martin gave a big sniff. "VALENTINE WAS SUCKED RIGHT INTO THE BOX! Last thing I saw was his face disappearing in a wisp of smoke! And...and...that's not all either," the hamster said, looking shiftily about. "Something very bad happened. Krispin said, 'One Beloved down, four more to go!' Knitbone – *he knows about us!*"

Knitbone paced round and round, up and down Winnie's bedroom, growling to himself, trying to make sense of the situation. How had this happened? Poor Valentine, what *was* he thinking? Questions batted about like a panicky moth trapped in a lampshade. It was going to take a lot of ginger biscuits to figure this one out.

One thing was certain, though; it looked like they had underestimated Krispin O'Mystery. They had written him off as a daft beardy-weirdy, but he was clearly very dangerous.

First thing the next morning, Knitbone, Martin, Gabriel and Orlando followed Krispin and Meryl to the pantry. They watched as Meryl collected every single pack of ginger biscuits and disposed of them in a black bin bag.

"Cunning so-and-sos are trying to starve us

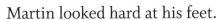

out!" hissed Gabriel. "Lucky for us Martin is such a hoarder. You've been stockpiling ginger biscuits in case of a rainy day, haven't you, Martin?"

Martin looked hard at his feet.

"*Haven't you, Martin?*" repeated Gabriel. Everybody looked at Martin and a strong smell of peppermint wafted around the room.

"Well, that's just great," sighed Knitbone, rolling his eyes to the ceiling.

"I've got a *few* packs left," protested Martin. "It's just that they are so delicious and I'm sure I'm still growing or something…"

Orlando was watching Krispin very carefully. As he swept out of the pantry, the outline of a box was visible in his coat pocket, its glass top just peeking out. "I see funny box in Fibbychop pocket," he whispered. "You see it too?"

Martin nodded eagerly. "Yup. That's definitely it."

"Good work," said Knitbone. "We've got to get hold of it and let Valentine out."

"But how are we supposed to do that?" asked Gabriel.

"We wait for right moment," said Orlando, narrowing his eyes and swinging his tail from side to side, excited by the prospect of an ambush. "You'll see, time will come. Naughty man wanna watch out."

In the ballroom, Krispin took the box from his pocket and threw his coat over a set of moose antlers above the fireplace. He stretched and yawned, plonking himself down in one of the Peppers' old armchairs. He placed the glass box safely on his lap and settled down for a snooze, muttering something to Meryl about her "not slacking".

Krispin needn't have bothered. Meryl was extremely busy fine-tuning the Ghost Locator-ator machine. She twiddled, she fiddled, she sighed and she tutted. Eventually, after she gave it a swift kick, it coughed and spluttered into life.

The Beloveds watched patiently from the sidelines, waiting for the perfect moment to perform the robbery. The conditions were ideal. The box was within easy reach, Meryl was busy and Krispin was fast asleep and snoring like a blocked drain.

"Pffft. Silly Fibbyface," tutted Orlando. "He make stealing spooky box easy-peasy. We do it right now."

"Wait a minute, Orlando," growled Knitbone. Something didn't seem quite right. It all seemed suspiciously easy, for a start. "Hang on…"

But Orlando wasn't listening. He flipped up onto the mantelpiece and then down onto the arm of Krispin's chair. "Orlando is a-comin', you cheeky monkey…"

Suddenly the compass on Meryl's machine began to spin wildly. It juddered and clicked as a paper strip spooled out of the side. Gabriel, Knitbone and Martin dashed over to look.

Gabriel read out the tiny words: "…*monkey business…monkey business…monkey business…*"

"WAIT! ORLANDO, STOP!" barked Knitbone. "IT'S A TRAP!"

"*NOW!*" cried Meryl.

Like an alligator, Krispin's eyes suddenly snapped wide open. From down the side of the armchair he pulled out a fistful of the shiniest silver spoons Orlando had ever seen, sending dazzling splinters of light around the room. The little monkey was bewitched for a moment,

trapped like a rabbit in headlights. Krispin deftly flipped the lid of the glass box, and – *whoosh* – Orlando was sucked inside as briskly as a button up a Hoover.

Trembling and in shock, Knitbone, Martin and Gabriel ran from the ballroom, up to the safety of the attic. They sat in silence, nibbling anxiously at Martin's rainy day supplies. Eyeing the small pile, it would seem that it was less of a rainy day he was saving for and more of a drizzly half an hour.

Everything was going very, very wrong. Something horribly strange was unfolding and the Beloveds were completely in the dark about it.

Once they'd calmed down, they decided on a low-profile stake-out to gather more information. The spooks crept back downstairs and took it in turns to watch Krispin's every move, scribbling down evidence in notebooks. As it happened, the notes were not that useful, as all they showed was that Krispin spent a lot of time gazing in the mirror, practising different expressions. When he wasn't doing this, he was either lecturing Meryl on his mystical abilities or picking his nose.

Finally, just when the spooks were beginning to despair of any information whatsoever, Krispin reached inside the pocket of his coat and brought out the dainty glass box. He fingered its shiny edges, held it close to his lips and whispered in a sinister baby voice, "Hello in there, you funny little ghosty-whosties, snug and cosy in my pretty Soul Box. You thought you were too clever for

Krispin O'Mystery, didn't
you? Where are your
other friends? The rat
and the duck? What
about that mongrel?
Wandering around
Starcross like they own
the place." Krispin's eyes
glittered greedily. "Stupid

Beloveds and their silly loyalty. You're used to
having everything your own way, aren't you? Well,
not any more. You need to be taught a lesson.
S.O.S., is it? We'll see about that. This place is
going to be mine. Soon I'll have you all trapped in
my little Soul Box. *Then* we'll see who's in charge."

Krispin put the box back safely in his pocket.
He clicked his fingers at Meryl, who stood up and
obediently followed him back to the bus for tea.
As he left the ballroom, he could be heard
announcing, "I've got plans for this place and

nobody's going to get in my way. Especially not *Knitbone Pepper*."

Knitbone gulped. *Krispin knew his actual name.* He felt very scared, but tried not to show it. Gabriel and Martin were openly wild-eyed with panic. They packed up their notebooks and pens and turned to leave. But as they did, they became aware of a buzzy sound.

"What's that?" said Martin, turning around. It was coming from underneath the armchair. It was Krispin's phone, forgotten and jumping around on the wooden floor. A picture flashed up on the screen of a sour-faced woman looking about as cheerful as a bulldog chewing on a nettle.

With his eyebrows up to his ears, Knitbone read the name on the screen out loud: "N O R A S O C K P U P P E T."

Nora Sockpuppet

Message
Kevin have u
trapped the
Starcros...

The Beloveds read the text together:

Kevin have u trapped the Starcross Stinkers
yet? Remember the deal. Starcross is perfect
location for Krispin's Krazy Haunted House.
At last, this is your chance to be a rich,
famous TV star. Don't blow it, little brother.
Call me.

Nora Sockpuppet? The Head Bossyboots of
Bartonshire Town Council was Krispin's *big sister*?
Now THIS really *was* news. Knitbone did a bit of
quick calculating.

$$(Starcross - The\ Peppers)$$
$$+ (Nora + Krispin)$$
$$= Oodles\ of\ Dodgy$$
$$Double\text{-}Dealing\ Dosh$$

Knitbone jumped in the air and woofed triumphantly. "I KNEW IT! This is a set-up! It's all a PLAN! The whole letter, debt and auction malarkey is all about one thing and one thing only: stealing Starcross from under our very noses to use as a location for a TV show! Krispin and Nora are in it together – Nora even knows about *us*!" The whole thing stank of trickery. It stank even more than when Lady Pepper found Knitbone's dead vole "present" inside her welly, and that *really* stank.

But that still didn't answer two very worrying questions: HOW did Krispin and Nora know about S.O.S.? And, if he was going to be hosting a television show about ghosts at Starcross Hall, *what did Krispin plan to do with its Beloveds*?

Chapter 14

Bolt From the Blue

Winnie was no idiot. She was good at maths, science, Monopoly and untangling Christmas lights. She was also an excellent judge of character and her instincts told her that Krispy O'Wotsit was up to no good. Unfortunately, he didn't look the sort to be put off by tales of damp and dodgy electrics so she decided to spy on him instead. She followed him around the house, keeping to the shadows.

He had some very odd habits and Winnie

suspected he might be as mad as a stoat. For example, on the first day, he had spent a long time staring into a dusty old Chinese vase, at one point stuffing pink wafer biscuits into it. Eventually she'd got fed up with trying to make sense of his bizarre behaviour and gone to bed.

The second day wasn't much better. It had been a very boring Saturday afternoon, hiding in the ballroom broom cupboard, listening to him banging on about how special he was. How Meryl put up with it, she didn't know. Winnie had tried taking notes, but all the entries in her notebook read something along the lines of: *My mystical blood runs true*, and, *My hair is the work of the angels*.

But the moment Krispin picked up that funny little glass box, his whole manner had changed. He became very focused and a greedy glint came into his eye. He looked really creepy. Winnie sat up and paid attention, peeking through the keyhole, straining to listen as he started talking.

And the news she heard shocked her to the core.

Winnie sat on the edge of her bed and pondered the enormity of the revelation.

If she understood correctly, Krispin O'Mystery seemed to believe that Knitbone was still here in Starcross. Could it be true? The very thought made Winnie's heart race.

She knew for a fact that Knitbone was dead, so that left only one other explanation, and that was as nutty as a squirrel's picnic.

Winnie was a very practical girl who didn't believe in spooky nonsense. She always believed that there was a sensible reason for bumps in the night. Only gibbering loonies like Krispin believed in ghosts, certainly not down-to-earth girls like Winnie Pepper.

But then again, if she *was* wrong, then lots of things started to make sense…

On the day that Knitbone died, Winnie couldn't bear to be with other people. She had run to her room and hidden in her wardrobe. There she sat in the gloom, scratching his name inside a heart into the floor, tears plopping onto the wooden boards. She hadn't told anybody about the heart, because it was a private thing. But after this, she had to admit that strange things had begun to happen.

Occasionally, Winnie thought she'd heard Knitbone, barking in the distance, and then a few weeks ago, she had looked out of the school bus window and, from far away, had been convinced that she had seen a dog waiting at the bus stop. Sometimes the end of her bed where Knitbone used to sleep definitely felt warm. Winnie had wanted him to be there so badly she thought she must have been imagining it. She even thought she'd heard funny scratching and bumping noises coming from the attic above her bedroom, but she knew that no one had been up there for years, so had told herself it was mice…

Actually, now she came to think of it, there had been plenty of clues. Why hadn't she noticed before?

The Bartonshire Times newspaper article! She

rushed downstairs, rescued it from the recycling bin and took it back up to her room, closing the door firmly and quietly behind her.

Smoothing out the creases, she looked at the headline again.

SPOOKY STARCROSS SPIRITS HAUNT HORRIFIED HOMEBUYERS!

She inspected the photograph closely. The grey smudge in the lower half of the picture next to her leg was just as she'd thought. Perhaps it was a finger mark on the lens, or a printing mistake… Whatever it was, there was no denying that it looked very much like *the shape of a dog*.

There were four other smudges too, but they were too faint to make out. She took out her magnifying glass and examined the strongest smudge again. What she saw made her gasp.

Right at the top of the smudge, where the

head should be, were two bright eyes staring back at her. She'd have recognized them anywhere.

The auction was tomorrow and the Peppers' future was uncertain. Winnie had nothing left to lose. It was time for a leap into the unknown.

Chapter 15

Dearly Beloved

Over in the corner of Winnie's bedroom, Knitbone sat in the wardrobe trying to figure things out. Nora Sockpuppet, TV shows, Krispin's scary weirdness – the day had been an exhausting one and he needed a bit of a rest. Martin and Gabriel sat sprawled on the rug playing cards and I-Spy.

Knitbone's favourite pastime these days was "Winnie Watching" and he found it very soothing. She was fascinating and he never, ever got bored.

Through a crack in the wardrobe door he watched her, deep in thought, her brow furrowed, nibbling at her nails.

What *was* she thinking about? She was reading the newspaper, so it might be a science project, or possibly history. She was *so* clever. He put his chin on his paws and gave a besotted sigh.

Winnie sprang to her feet and crossed over to her dressing table. Knitbone's ears pricked up. *Now* what was she doing?

Winnie opened the bottom drawer and took out a wooden box. She sat with it on her lap for a minute, almost as if she was reluctant to open it. This was intriguing. Martin and Gabriel stopped what they were doing and watched too.

Taking a silver key from around her neck, Winnie turned it in the little lock, lifted the lid and took out its contents. It was a bit grubby, a bit chewed and a bit old, but there was no doubting who it belonged to. With a jolt, Knitbone recognized it straight away.

"Knitbone," said Martin, putting his cards down, "isn't that your old collar? The one with the pumpkins on it?"

Winnie held the collar and closed her eyes. She took a deep breath and whispered three small words that Knitbone had never expected to hear again: "Come here, boy."

Knitbone reeled in shock. He didn't know what to do, so he did nothing. His head began to buzz and his mind filled with stars. He had waited for this moment for so long and now he felt stuck to the floor, as if his feet were painted with glue.

"Heavens to Betsy!" Gabriel started beating his wings and honking delightedly. "She knows you're here! Knitbone, get out of the wardrobe!" Martin jumped up and down on the spot clapping his little hands…

Unaware of the fuss going on around her, Winnie waited in silence for something to happen. Perhaps she hadn't said it clearly enough? Maybe ghosts couldn't hear that well. She was new to this after all. She took a deep breath and said it again, only a bit louder: "Come here, boy."

"Come on, Knitbone, lad, what are you waiting for?" honked Gabriel. "What if this is your only chance to reunite? You can do it!"

Knitbone stared through the crack, as if in a trance.

Martin squeezed himself through the gap in the wardrobe door. "This might be your moment! Snap out of it! Now!" There was only one thing for it. "Sorry about this," shouted the hamster as he slapped Knitbone smartly around the face. "Focus, Knitbone, focus!"

Knitbone tried with all his might, willing her to see him. He closed the door and concentrated very, very hard, remembering their days in the sun, chasing bees and jumping over hay bales. He remembered pulling a giggling baby Winnie in a little red truck. He remembered her first day at school. But now his head was all swimmy and he felt woozy…

Winnie felt hot tears pricking her eyes. Nothing was happening and she was starting to feel silly. If he was here, then why wasn't he answering? She thought she would try one more time.

"Knitbone Pepper, Starcross home-grown and BFF, if you can hear me, *please, let me know.*" By now Gabriel's eyes were nearly popping out of their sockets. "KNITBONE,

YOU DAFT HOUND.
CAN'T YOU SEE
WE'RE LOSING
HER! IT'S NOW OR
NEVER! DOOOO
SOMETHING!"

It was all too much for Martin, who was back on the rug, his head between his knees, taking deep, calming breaths.

Knitbone tried with all his might. He heaved and he puffed and he blew, but he didn't even know if he was doing it right. If only he had some instructions.

He tried to say, "Winnie, hang on! I'm over here!" but his words sounded as if they were coming from far, far away…

The clock ticked on the wall and the birds sang outside. Lord Pepper's voice rang out from the kitchen, calling Winnie for dinner. It was a picture of ordinariness and normality.

"So, that's that," murmured Winnie. "It was a stupid idea all along." But she had *so* wanted it to be true. Warm salty tears rolled down her cheeks, spilling onto her knees and making little sploshes. It obviously wasn't destined to be. She pulled her jumper sleeve over her hands and wiped her eyes. "Oh, Knitbone," she said sadly. "I am a stupid girl. *Of course* you're not here any more."

Winnie caught sight of the sad-looking girl in her dressing table mirror. Poor Winnie Pepper, silly enough to believe in ghosts and soon to be homeless. What a pathetic picture she made.

"Winnieeee, dinnneeerrr!"

"I'm not hungry any more," she called down the stairs in reply, holding in a sob. "Maybe later."

Winnie felt in her pocket for a hanky, but all she found was an old sweet and some bits of fluff. She fingered Knitbone's collar again. "I *wish* Krispin would go away. I *wish* we didn't have to sell Starcross. But most of all, Knitbone Pepper, I *wish* you were still here."

She put the collar back in its box, sniffed and stood up. Winnie realized she'd better hurry up and dry her eyes, otherwise there would be questions when she went downstairs. She remembered there was a new box of birthday hankies somewhere in her wardrobe, so she trudged over to the other side of the room and pulled wide the creaky wooden door.

As she did so, something soft tumbled silently out onto the rug. Winnie clapped a hand over her mouth to hold in a scream. Her heart beating loudly in her chest, she dared to look closer. It looked like a big dandelion clock, at least at first. Soon, she could see darker fluffy bits, then some scrubby bits, then gradually something that looked like a shiny nose, and then eyes…eyes that twinkled like the brightest stars.

Knitbone bounded up into Winnie's arms, his heart as light as a cloud. Winnie was so happy, she thought she'd died and gone to Heaven.

"I'm SOOO pleased to see you, it's just been *awful* without you." She hugged him tight. It was a bit like hugging candyfloss, only much, much better. Once Winnie had acclimatized to

Knitbone's new form, she suddenly discovered that she was also looking at two other animals.

"Who's that behind you? Is that a goose? Goodness, isn't that the goose from the portrait in the library? And a little hamster! Why is he holding his tummy in?"

Knitbone explained everything whilst Winnie sat on her bed and listened, grinning happily.

"Well, it's a pleasure to make your acquaintances," she said at the end, smiling at the goose and the hamster. She kissed Knitbone on the tip of his nose and was tousling his fur when a thought suddenly struck her. She stopped mid-ruffle. "Wait a minute..." Winnie's mouth hung open in amazement. She pointed her finger at Knitbone and stared at him wide-eyed. "Did you just...*TALK*?" Winnie laughed in disbelief. "Well I never! You're very good at growling your R's. You've even got a bit of a Bartonshire accent!"

"I *am* Starcross home-grown you know," said Knitbone sheepishly. "Talking's one of the perks of being a ghost. That and being able to read, of course."

"READ?!" exclaimed Winnie, reeling in astonishment. "Are you telling me you can READ?"

"That's the thing about being dead," woofed Knitbone cheerfully. "You win some, you lose some."

"Wow." Winnie, deep in thought, nibbled at the end of her plait. "This is a lot to take in. So, you're my Beloved. I like the sound of that. I wish I'd known before. We can do lots of fun things together again. S.O.S. sounds like an excellent organization… It certainly explains the mystery of why we always seem to be running out of ginger biscuits and teaspoons…" Winnie hesitated, took a deep breath and then it all came out in a rush. "Listen, Knitbone, I've got something to tell you. Whilst you've been gone, everything has gone wrong. I've got some very bad news about the house. It's going to be sold. Tomorrow. I'm SO sorry."

Knitbone rolled his eyes and woofed. "We already know, Winnie. Who do you think has been behind all the hauntings?"

Winnie giggled with relief, but stopped abruptly as a terrible thought occurred to her. "So if we have to leave Starcross, you *will* all be able to come with us, won't you?"

There was a pause. Knitbone couldn't bear to tell her the difficult truth.

"Won't you? You will, won't you, Knitbone?"

He whined and put his head in her lap.

"Oh no! But...I've only just found you again, and we're nearly out of time!" Winnie's eyes welled up with tears.

Gabriel stepped forward. "Miss Winnie, please don't worry. We're not going to let that happen."

He spat on his wing tip and held it out. "Please accept our official invitation to become an honorary recruit. Welcome to S.O.S.!"

Chapter 16

The Sockpuppet Scam

The O'Mystery bus was parked next to the hedge. It was a golden, balmy evening, and Krispin and Meryl were relaxing under a patchwork bus-awning. Bells and windchimes dangled from its fringed edges and a woven zig-zag Turkish rug lay on the ground. A laptop computer rested on a small table, plinky-plonky-twinkle music tinkling out of it.

Krispin, wearing a constipated expression and lycra leggings, was doing yoga whilst chanting

"*Ommmm*". Meryl was doing a crossword on the steps of the bus, furrowing her brow and chewing a pencil. Both were completely unaware that Knitbone, Winnie, Gabriel and Martin were hiding in the hedge, watching their every move.

The Soul Box sat near Krispin on the rug, its insides swirling with a grey smoke. Occasionally it rocked from side to side, as if its occupants were trying to get out.

Martin, sitting on top of Knitbone's head, pointed a twig at it. "*Look* – it's Orlando and Valentine!" he whispered. "It looks very squashed in there."

A sudden loud ringing from the computer made Knitbone jump. Martin fell off his head with a squeak and landed in a pile of leaves.

Krispin leaped up and grabbed the laptop. "Nozza!" he exclaimed cheerfully as he pressed a button, before sitting back down again, cross-legged, his back to the hedge.

Nora Sockpuppet's expressionless eyes stared out of the screen. She was sitting in her council office, surrounded by dead pot plants. "There you are," she grumbled flatly, folding her arms. "I've been trying to get hold of you all afternoon. Why don't you answer your phone?"

Krispin patted his hair. "I've been busy catching the rabbit thing and the monkey. Don't worry, I know what I'm doing. I *am* a professional, you know."

Nora humphed. "You *are* going to be able to catch them all, aren't you? Because if you can't, they are going to make your life a nightmare. Especially that mongrel."

"Calm down, Nora," soothed Krispin. "I'll have them all in my little Soul Box before you can say 'Exterminator'." He tutted loudly and rolled his eyes. "Ghost hunters know *all* about Beloveds – it's one of the first things you learn in training." He took a textbook from his yoga bag and flipped it open, quoting from the pages. "'*A Beloved is the most loyal sort of ghost. Fiercely protective of their home and people, their devotion should not be underestimated.*'" He slammed the book shut. "It's typical that they *would* be animals of course: dirty, stupid things. Trapping and disposal is the only option." He nodded at the glass box on the patterned rug.

"Disposal?" sniffed Nora. "What does that mean exactly?"

"Oh, you know," said Krispin, waving his hand breezily. "They'll be dissolved; every trace of their existence destroyed… Horribly painful and rather messy. You wouldn't think you could murder a ghost, but the *Double-Dedder* move is surprisingly straightforward when you know how."

The privet leaves on the hedge trembled.

"Finding the spider in that Chinese vase *was* a bit of luck! What a traitorous loner Mrs Jones turned out to be." Krispin cackled with laughter. "She was a goldmine of useful insider information, spilling the beans about this place and its ghosts – all for a few pink wafer biscuits."

Knitbone looked gobsmacked. "*Mrs Jones?*" he whispered incredulously. "As in Mrs Jones, *the spider?*" Gabriel's beak dropped open in shock. Martin took a small piece of ginger biscuit out of his cheek. (He'd been saving it for a difficult moment exactly like this.)

Krispin sighed deeply then smiled. "I do *love* a Bad Egg. You can always rely on them to let the side down."

At this bit of spite, Nora appeared to cheer up. "I knew Starcross would be perfect. It's been virtually untouched for centuries. Plus everybody knows the Peppers are broke – they never pay their bills on time." Her little eyes glittered.

Krispin reached inside his yoga bag again and pulled out a document. He waved it at the screen.

"What's that?" hissed Knitbone. "Wossit say?"

"*Krispin's Krazy Haunted House*," Gabriel whispered, craning his long neck. "It's got signatures at the bottom. It's some sort of contract. Shhh – listen."

Krispin smacked a big kiss on the bundle of papers. "This TV deal is worth two million pounds and I've just signed on the dotted line. It's *great* having the Head of Bartonshire Town Council for a big sister! If Starcross Hall hadn't have been on your patch, I'd never have known about it. The TV company will love it – ancient, tumbledown yet majestic, brimming with spookiness. And now it's even got a ghostly reputation. We've struck pure ghost gold. At last, I'm going to be the mega-famous, insanely-rich media star I've always deserved to be."

At this thought Krispin made a pouty, sulky face and pounded his fist on the small table. "Nora, why isn't Starcross mine already? It should be *all* mine. I want it NOW."

Nora frowned and folded her arms again. "Don't be a half-wit, Kevin. I explained this to you already. A 'Seize and Sell' auction is council procedure. We have to do it this way otherwise it looks as dodgy as a daffodil sausage. We don't want people poking around in our business, pointing fingers, getting suspicious that I rigged the whole thing, do we?"

Knitbone and Winnie looked at each other, open-mouthed in shock. Disgusted, Gabriel blew silent raspberries, whilst Martin clenched his little fists and shook them furiously.

Completely unaware of the outraged audience in the hedge, Krispin continued to sulk and twiddle his pointy beard. "But what if someone else tries to buy it tomorrow at the auction? I couldn't *bear* it if somebody else got it."

Nora sighed. "Kevin, *nobody else wants it.* At the start, I thought I might have to scare people off myself, but seeing as that awful Pepper kid and those creepy critters have made it about as desirable as a slug sandwich, we'll be able to buy it on the cheap."

Winnie pulled rude faces, whilst Knitbone flattened his ears and bared his teeth.

"By the way," Krispin guffawed, "I've found a talent agency called *Broken Spirits* and I've got big plans for the show. I'm going to employ nice, well-behaved *human* ghosts and introduce a new one every week as part of my act. *These* ghosts know what's good for them, unlike *some* I could mention. Anxious monks doing card tricks, cowering juggling servants, timid dancing milkmaids… Audiences won't be able to get enough of it. I'll feed them chocolate biscuits to make them sleepy and keep them quiet. They'll do exactly as they are told and I'll look *amazing*. It's essential that the bothersome Beloveds don't get in my way. Out with the old, in with the new."

Nora raised a big hairy eyebrow. "So when EXACTLY are you going to catch the others?"

"Later tonight. I'm staging a séance. You know I *love* a show. It'll be a Grand Finale. Don't worry,

I've got all of the right traps so it'll be easy-peasy. There are only three of them left, and they'll be as weak as kittens without their ginger biscuits." Krispin shuddered. "Animal ghosts – what a vile idea. Why anyone would want a pet is beyond me, never mind a *dead one* of all things. Yuck."

He turned and barked at Meryl. "OI! You like animals, don't you?" She looked up from her crossword and nodded. Krispin leaned into his screen and whispered to Nora, "It's one of her many weaknesses."

Nora yawned, exposing broken teeth like castle ruins. "Well, time for my beauty sleep. Not long to go now. Within twenty-four hours, Starcross Hall will be yours. Nighty-night."

"Night-night, Nora."

Krispin pressed another button on his laptop, and Nora's face vanished. He dropped the Soul Box into his yoga bag. "The pathetic Peppers are about to have their home stolen from right under their noses, and they don't even have a clue." Krispin stepped over to Meryl, whipped her crossword away and tore it into little pieces.

"Right," growled Knitbone, back in the safety of the attic. He was pointing a stick at a complicated diagram of Starcross Hall. "As you can see, *here*, *here* and *here* we have A Very Big Problem. The Sockpuppets have stitched us up good and proper. Ideas, anybody? Yes," he woofed, pointing at Gabriel. "You."

"*Me?!*" Startled, Gabriel looked around at the others. "No, not a sausage. No ideas at all! I was hoping someone else would know what to do."

Martin waved his hand in the air excitedly. "Oooh! Oooh! I know! We could barricade ourselves in the house and not let anyone in. Ever."

"But I have to go to school at some point," protested Winnie gently.

Martin climbed up her jumper and looked her straight in the eye. "Are you sure about that? To be honest, we'd rather you didn't."

Then Knitbone had an idea that was so bright it should have had its own lampshade.

"I think," he said slowly, "that we might be able to play Krispin at his own game."

"What do you mean?" asked Gabriel.

"He thinks there are only three of us, doesn't he? He doesn't know about Winnie being on board yet. That makes four…and *maybe* we could fool him into thinking there are even *more* of us!" Knitbone woofed excitedly and ran in a little circle, thoughts racing. "The séance would be the ideal backdrop for a showdown…yes… Starcross

Stinkers, Nora called us? We'll give them Starcross Stinkers, alright! If it's a Grand Finale Krispin O'Mystery wants, then a Grand Finale is exactly what Krispin O'Mystery is *going to get*."

The ghosts planned, plotted, hatched, conspired and concocted until, eventually, midnight was nearly upon them.

"Are you *sure* we should eat all those pink wafers?" asked Martin doubtfully, eyeing the towering sugary pile in front of them.

"Yes," said Knitbone. "Ginger biscuits are all very well, but pink wafer biscuits will give us that extra boost."

"I thought the Handy Tips and Hints handout said that they made us *extremely naughty*?"

"Well, we need to be *extremely naughty* tonight, don't we?" Knitbone replied, cocking his ear to one side cheekily. "Plus Krispin thinks we've run out of ginger biscuits, so he'll expect us to be a bit useless."

"So we'll have the element of wafery surprise, you mean?"

"Exactly, Martin. Now, have you sorted out the ropes?"

"Check."

"Super-stinks?"

"Check."

"Gabriel, you're on electrics, fittings and explosives."

"Check."

"Winnie, you're on the Soul Box."

Winnie put her thumbs up and grinned. "Check."

"Right, everybody," Knitbone woofed loudly and proudly. "Remember: we're in it to win it. It's time to show Krispin who's in charge round here." With this the remaining Beloveds and Winnie joined hands, paws and wings, chanting as one.

"For the Peppers! For Starcross! *For heart and home!*"

Chapter 17

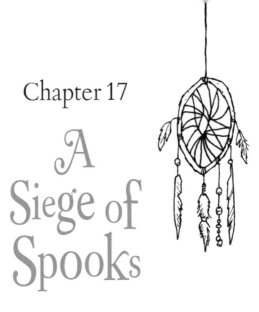

A Siege of Spooks

Krispin and his drippy fans were getting ready to begin the séance in the ballroom. They wore a lot of floaty clothing and jingly jewellery. The large chandelier had been turned down, candles flickered and some of Lady Pepper's best silk headscarves were draped over the table lamps. (Krispin was big on atmosphere.)

Krispin O'Mystery was looking very theatrical. He was wearing a long velvet cloak embroidered with stars, and had sprayed sparkly stuff in his hair.

His hands were adorned with enough crystal rings to fill a market stall and he had gone overboard on the eyeliner.

He looked at the clock; it was one minute to midnight. Everything was in place. Everything except for one very important thing: the Soul Box.

After some frantic searching, Krispin realized that he had left it back on the bus. Immensely frustrated, he growled at Meryl to go and fetch it straight away. Meryl stuck out her bottom lip defiantly and pushed her glasses up her nose. "But I need to stay with the Ghost Locator-ator."

Krispin glanced over at the machine in the corner, plugged in and humming contentedly. "It's rather tricky if you're not trained," she mumbled defensively.

"Don't be a ninny, *MERYL*, just DO IT," Krispin hissed out of the corner of his mouth. "I'm about to start, so you better be quicker than a racehorse on rollerskates!"

Meryl shuffled out of the room just as the clock on the mantlepiece chimed midnight. Krispin took a deep, steadying breath and smoothed down his hair. At last the time had come: the final bagging of the Beloveds was about to begin.

"Welcome, everyone," he boomed. "Please sit and join hands to make a *Circle of Spookiness*." With great solemnity, arms were outstretched and linked in a general jingle of bangles around a circular dining table. Krispin raised his chin and his eyes went all wobbly, like a couple of underdone eggs. "Spirits, we are ready for you. If you can hear, knock twice." A few moments passed and then…

KNOCK KNOCK.

There was a shriek of terror. The door creaked open and the candles blew out as Lord Pepper popped his head round the door. "Goodness, are you all still up? I was just looking for my glasses.

It's terribly dark in here, how can you see anything?" He turned the lights on and everybody tutted. "Oh, dear," he said, looking round apologetically, "have I interrupted something?"

"Lord Pepper," growled Krispin through gritted teeth. "We are very busy contacting the spirits, so kindly GO AWAY." Lord Pepper looked relieved to be excused and made a quick exit, closing the door behind him.

Krispin settled himself back into his chair and calmed himself. The group all joined hands and the Circle of Spookiness began again.

"As I said before, *is anybody there?*" A few seconds passed. Then the lights began to judder, flickering on and off. Krispin looked delighted. "Aha, I see there is. Come forward, Spirit."

Gabriel's voice was not as powerful as when he was alive, but the exercises had definitely made his honk louder. In addition to this, Winnie had made Gabriel a loudspeaker cone out of an old Christmas card. Through this he could make a range of suitably spooky sounds. He leaned into it with his beak and gave it his all.

"WoOoOoOo! LEAVE THIS PLAAAACE!" he boomed. "KRISPIN O'MYSTERY, YOU ARE A BAD, BAD MAN, AND YOU ARE NOT WANTED HERE!"

Krispin smiled in a knowing manner. "Now, now, Spirit, there's no need to be rude. Introduce yourself. Are you, perchance, *Martin*, from the Second World War? Perhaps you are *Gabriel*, from the time of Charles the First?" His brow darkened. "Or are you *Knitbone Pepper*?"

"NO. MY NAME IS…" Gabriel faltered, reading the side of the Christmas card. "…RUDOLPH!"

"Rudolph?" Krispin looked baffled. Mrs Jones hadn't mentioned anything about a *Rudolph*. "So, Rudolph, what is your last name?"

"THE REINDEER."

"Rudolph the Reindeer," said Krispin flatly, arching a doubtful eyebrow. "Really?"

"ER…YES, AND WE DON'T LIKE YOU OR YOUR WEIRDY-BEARDY FRIENDS. LEAVE NOW AND YOU

WILL BE FREE TO GO. STAY AND *TERRIBLE THINGS* SHALL BEFALL YOU ALL."

"Well," said Krispin, matter-of-factly, "I think I'll take my chances, *Rudolph*, because you don't sound particularly scary."

"I AM."

"Well, you don't sound it."

"WELL, I AM, THOUGH."

Suddenly a blood-curdling scream came from overhead as Martin launched himself from the chandelier. He was painted head to foot in red chilli-sauce warpaint and was swinging his sword savagely around his head. Squealing and squeaking like a crazed thing, he hurled himself onto Krispin's back and stabbed furiously at his shoulder with his tiny sword. "DIE, KRISPIN O'MYSTERY! DIE!" Martin had eaten a lot of pink wafers.

"OW!" Alarmed, Krispin stood up and tried to bat him off. "OW! That really hurts! GERROFF!"

As Gabriel grew in confidence, he experimented with a new voice, high and screechy this time. "There's meeee tooooo. My name is… um…*Zelda*…and I am the ghost of an angry owl. Twit-twOoOoOo!" Gabriel passed Knitbone the cone and swooped down on Krispin, battering him around the head with invisible wings.

"Zelda? Who's *Zelda*?" protested Krispin, thrashing wildly at thin air. "Mrs Jones never mentioned a Zelda!"

Now it was Knitbone's turn. He growled menacingly into the loudspeaker, "I AM THE GHOST OF A SAVAGE, MURDEROUS BEAR!

MY NAME IS ANDREW." A large potted plant toppled over with a crash.

"A *bear*? Er…savage, murderous bear, please stay calm," Krispin bleated meekly, noticing with alarm that portraits of long-dead ancestors were beginning to rotate slowly on the walls. His followers had begun to stand up from the table, gathering round him, or edging towards the door. Krispin tried to look humble. "Whoever you are, Spirits, I mean you no harm."

"DON'T LIE TO ME, KRISPIN O'MYSTERY!" Andrew sounded wild with rage. "LIARS AND CHEATS MAKE US ALL MAD! GRRRRRRR!"

"All? How many of you *are* there?" frowned Krispin, getting to his feet, pushing his followers away.

Martin scampered up onto Krispin's shoulder and shouted down his earhole,

"I am a vicious boggit!" Then he bit his ear like it was a delicious ham toastie.

"AARRGGH! Stop it! Stop it!" Krispin bellowed. "Where's Meryl? *MERYYYL!*" The enormous, cut-glass chandelier suddenly crashed to the floor, a blizzard of crystal hail, pieces flying everywhere.

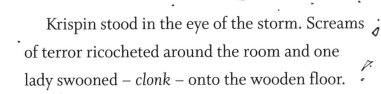

Krispin stood in the eye of the storm. Screams of terror ricocheted around the room and one lady swooned – *clonk* – onto the wooden floor.

Knitbone slammed windows open and shut as the sound of screaming, crashing and banging escalated. Old tapestries flapped around the room like giant moth-eaten bats, propelled on Gabriel's wings, swooping down and swiping at the audience.

With his back legs, Knitbone kangaroo-kicked over a suit of armour with a clatter, exploding it into a dozen pieces.

He took hold of an axe in his teeth, spinning round and round, letting it fly across the ballroom and land – *THUD* – in the wall, centimetres above Krispin's head. "EEK!" Krispin squealed. "THAT – Andrew, Zelda, vicious boggit, or *whoever* you are – was very DANGEROUS!"

Followers clung to each other in terror, eyes as round as saucers, skin as pale as milk. A grey-haired woman clutched at her beads and shrieked, "You're supposed to be a professional, Krispin! Make it stop!"

With this, scrawled words began to gradually emerge on the wall, daubed in blood by an invisible hand. (It was actually red ink from Winnie's art cupboard, and Knitbone was doing the writing with his tail.)

Starcross will NEVER belong to you!
We know what you are up to Kevin!
You and Nora have been RUMBLED
the secret's out!

"Kevin?" The grey-haired woman pointed shakily at the wall. "Who's Kevin? And what does it mean, you've been 'rumbled'?"

An elderly man clutched at his nose with a handkerchief, tears streaming down his face. "Good heavens… WHAT IS THAT TERRIBLE SMELL?!" It was reminiscent of boiled cabbage, kippers, Stilton cheese and wet dog, with top notes of angry skunk. It was so bad it gave off its own heat shimmer.

"Calm down, everyone, don't upset your chakras. Everything's under control," screeched Krispin, blocking his nostrils. Suddenly, his trouser buttons mysteriously popped off and dropped to his ankles, revealing pink, polka-dot underwear.

Krispin O'Mystery wasn't just out of his depth, he was drowning.

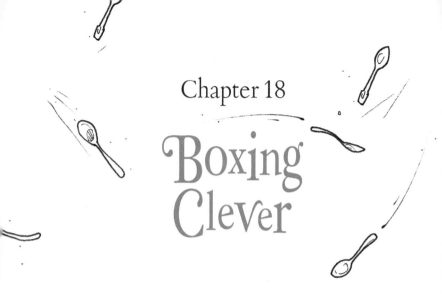

Chapter 18

Boxing Clever

While all the hullabaloo was going on in the ballroom, Winnie was busy breaking into the O'Mystery bus by moonlight. From a distance, she had spotted the Soul Box through the bus window, forgotten on a shelf, giving off a ghostly glow. She seized her chance. Poor Orlando and Valentine – she was going to set them free and get rid of that box once and for all. She crept under the awning and up the stairs, and pulled the curtain quietly to one side.

Inside the bus it reeked horribly of incense and hairspray. The walls were studded with photographs of almost-famous people wearing hunted expressions, Krispin clinging on to their arms. Newspaper clippings adorned the walls of the bus with titles such as "*Krispin is Kool*", "*That's the Spirit!*" and "*A Ghost of a Chance*".

Winnie held her nose and tried to focus on the job in hand. She slipped down the aisle and quietly reached up to the shelf, her fingers wrapping silently around the box. *Bingo,* she thought with a smile, and turned to leave.

"Can I help you?"

Winnie spun round to meet Meryl's accusing stare, her eyebrows wriggling and wiggling like caterpillars doing the tango.

"Ah, Meryl!" Winnie had forgotten about Meryl. "Ah…it's actually really good that you're here because…because…"

215

"Because I can stop you stealing things
that don't belong to you?"

"This? *Me?* Ha ha, no! I wasn't stealing this,
I was just…looking…for…"

Meryl sighed and pushed her glasses up her
nose. "You know what? Just take it."

"What?"

"Take it. It'll serve Krispin right. He treats me

like a worm, and his sister's a mean old witch too. It's about time I stood up for myself."

"Good for you, Meryl. Thanks!" Winnie made a dash for the exit, but turned at the last minute. "But what will you do now?"

"I'm going to train to be an accountant. I was never cut out for this sort of thing really. I like numbers in spreadsheets, not ghosts in bed sheets. Good luck."

Back in the ballroom, to Krispin's horror, the ghostly mayhem was gaining momentum.

Gabriel had set up a series of explosions using old fireworks that he'd found left over from Bonfire Night. Whizzes, bangs and pops ricocheted off the picture rails and coloured sparks sputtered overhead. Rockets squealed and Catherine wheels spun out of control. Firecrackers hopped about inside the grand piano, creating an orchestral racket of symphonic proportions.

Howling and clambering over each other in panic, Krispin's followers frantically tried to escape as Martin chased after them, gleefully stuffing fistfuls of nettles down their pants, giggling, "I'm a sting-y ghost-bee, BUZZZZ-BUZZZZ!"

"LOOK!" wailed a woman, shakily pointing her finger at the moose's head on the wall. "It's possessed!" Wired to the electrics, its eyes glowed red as Gabriel sat astride its antlers, honking through his loudspeaker, "I'M BRUCE THE MOOSE, GET OOT OF MY HOOSE!"

Knitbone was busy putting Winnie's catapult to good use, firing spoons from Orlando's collection, shooting them like silver bullets from his teeth. *Ping!*

"OW!" *Ping!* "OW! Not the *face!*" yelled Krispin, his arms raised, shielding himself from the blizzard of cutlery.

Without Meryl, the Ghost Locator-ator machine was going completely loopy. It shook like a dodgy spin-dryer. Steam shot out of random holes and its thermometer exploded. Paper spewed, then stuttered out of the side as it fell apart under the pressure: *DANGER… DONGER…PINGER…POOPER…*

Krispin was shaking with rage and fear. "Meryl! *MERYL!*" he shrieked. "I need the Soul Box NOW! Where *ARE* you, you useless woman? I'll have your guts for garters!"

He had one weapon left. Krispin clambered up onto the table and shook his fist angrily at the ceiling, his composure deserting him as quickly as his followers.

"Knitbone Pepper of Starcross Hall, you 'orrible little mutt, hear me now. I *know* you are in this room. *Lord knows* I have been patient with you, but now you give me no choice. You've asked for it! I'm going to finish you off – the time has come for *The Dog Whisper Trap*!"

Krispin tore a silver locket out of his shirt. He opened it with great drama and thrust it into the air.

Silence.

Nothing seemed to be happening and Gabriel and Martin started sniggering. What a numpty.

"Can you hear that?" said Knitbone suddenly, dropping the catapult with a clang.

"What?" The duo promptly stopped laughing.

"*That.* That sound? You must be able to hear it. It sounds like singing, like mermaids and birds and bells. Now it sounds like squirrels singing about sausages, butter and…socks…"

"NO! Knitbone – stop it! Don't listen, it's a trick." Panicking, Gabriel tried to cover Knitbone's wonky ears with his wings.

Knitbone pushed him away and drifted peacefully towards Krispin.

"Are you listening, Knitbone Pepper?" coaxed Krispin in a sing-song voice. "The whispers are calling you."

"It's soooo beautiful," moaned Knitbone dreamily. "Like sunlight and snowflakes and liver-flavoured dog treats…"

"KNITBONE, NO!" Gabriel and Martin were beside themselves with panic. Without Knitbone they were lost.

"Good boy, Knitbone Pepper, come on, come *he-re*, there's a good boy," cajoled Krispin in a sinister voice. "Nearly there…"

Suddenly the door exploded open. Winnie flew into the room, plaits flying and eyes blazing. She gripped the edge of the dining table and shoved it over, sending Krispin sailing across the room. He landed heavily on the floor, snapping the locket tight shut and squashing it as flat as a pancake.

"I've got it! I've got it!" shouted Winnie triumphantly, holding the Soul Box high above her head. "And now, *Kevin Sockpuppet*, I'M GOING TO FINISH IT!" She hurled the glass box down hard onto the marble hearth of the fireplace. As it shattered, smashing into a thousand glass splinters, a rush of smoke wooshed out, and with it came Orlando and Valentine.

"Phew! Hot as big badger's armpit in funny box," said Orlando grumpily, swinging his tail and leaping onto Knitbone's head.

Valentine unfolded his ears and shook out his legs. "Did I miss anything?"

Knitbone stopped and blinked, as if waking up from a dream. "Winnie, Orlando *and* Valentine!" he woofed delightedly. "Excellent work!'

Krispin lay face down having a tantrum, battered and bruised, pounding his fists on the floor. "It's not FAIR! I caught them fair and square. Bloomin' Beloveds! Starcross Stinkers! Ruining EVERYTHING!"

Orlando sprang off Knitbone, sprinted across the top of the picture frames, down a curtain and seized Krispin's wig in a tiny foot.

Scampering away, he squealed with joy. "Eez knitty-kitty keepsake for Orlando! Nice for spoons to sleep in."

Krispin clutched at his shiny bald head and wailed, "That's it, I'm leaving. But I'm not finished with you, you…you…*PEPPERS*! Don't think I am! What Kevin Sockpuppet wants, Kevin GETS."

He stomped from the ballroom, down the corridor and out of Starcross Hall, climbed into his bus and screeched away in a cloud of dust and exhaust fumes, closely followed by his band of straggling fans, feverishly clutching their tents and crystal balls, trying to keep up.

"How's THAT for a Grand Finale?" honked Gabriel out of the ballroom window. "I'd have thought you knew the old showbiz saying: 'never work with children and animals'!"

Winnie and the spooks danced around the wreckage of the room and hugged each other. They jumped for joy, they whooped, cheered and did a conga. "We did it! We scared him away!" woofed Knitbone, his tail wagging joyfully.

"I bet he wishes he'd never heard of Starcross Hall," beamed Martin, thrashing his sword about. "I hope the pink wafers wear off soon, though," he added ruefully. "I could do with a lie-down."

"Phew," sighed a relieved Winnie. "At last. Each and every one of the buyers has been scared away. Well done, everybody. I couldn't have managed it without you."

Orlando teetered, one-legged, on top of an abandoned crystal ball that had rolled on to the floor. He pretended to fall into a hypnotic trance, perching the wig on his head and crossing his eyes. "I'm Krispy O'Fibbychops!" the monkey squeaked, as the others giggled until their tummies ached. "I predict that tomorrow's auction," he announced, "will be massive flip-flop!"

Chapter 19

A Ghost of a Chance

Knitbone Pepper woke up in his wardrobe with a start. Winnie, her forehead pressed to her bedroom window, was looking down at the Starcross courtyard in despair. "But it's full of cars!" she wailed. "Nobody is supposed to be here. Knitbone, *why* is it full of cars?"

The sleepy Beloveds hurried to the window and looked down at the Bartonshire crowds. It was true; the courtyard was buzzing with cars and people. "I don't understand," said Winnie, turning to look at the others in bewilderment. "Why are they all here? They can't want to buy our house – everyone knows it's horribly haunted!"

Knitbone scrutinized the crowd and realized that he recognized some of them from when he had been alive. He spotted the butcher, the bus driver, the library lady and the nice vet that smelled of dog biscuits and cats. People were patting Lord and Lady Pepper on the back, shaking hands and heads, giving them cards and little gifts. The postman gave them a home-made cake. The old lady from the local shop gave them a bunch of flowers.

"Winnie, I don't think they're here to bid on the house," Knitbone woofed, wagging his tail. "I think they're here to show us that they *care*."

Martin sniffed very loudly and wiped his nose. Gabriel said he thought he might have something in his eye. Winnie gave Knitbone a big hug and they all made their way downstairs.

The auction room was packed. Of course, a few people were there hoping to pick up a bargain stuffed fox or a brace of Georgian pistols, but most of the visitors had indeed come to show their support. The local people of Bartonshire felt sad, because they knew that Peppers belonged at Starcross, and that Starcross belonged to the Peppers. It really was a disgrace and a crying shame. Bartonshire wouldn't be the same without them and their eccentric ways – it was the end of an era.

The auctioneer adjusted his glasses and rapped his gavel down to get everyone's attention.

"Right now, ladies and gentlemen. This morning you have the opportunity to buy a magnificent country house, built in AD 1109. It has been in the Pepper family for over 900 years and this is its first time on the market."

Lord Pepper stared at the floor, misery filling his boots. He was so distraught that he hadn't even been able to choose the right hat for the occasion. Lady Pepper dabbed at his tears with a beret.

Suddenly, Knitbone, peeping round the door, spotted two figures dressed in black, huddled together at the back of the room. His heart sank. "Oh NO! What are *THEY* doing here?" he howled. To his horror, Krispin and Nora were perched grimly on chairs, clutching their auction cards and gritting their teeth. "Oh, no no NoooOOOOOO!"

Winnie was filled with panic. "But I thought we'd scared them off! This is a disaster – they're harder to get rid of than chickenpox!"

The only consolation was that they looked extremely unhappy. Krispin seemed to have developed a noticeable twitch in his left eye and a wild, rolling look in the other one. It looked like he was determined to buy the house, ghosts or no ghosts. "I HAVE to have Starcross, Nora. I NEED it," he spat, cracking his knuckles one by one. "They can't stop me from buying it. I've got two million pounds of TV dosh and all those losers have is a ghostly grudge. When it's mine I'll hunt them down. They'll wish they *were* dead."

Nora grimaced and picked at some stray spinach in her teeth. "You really are an idiot, Kevin," she muttered irritably. "At this rate we'll pick it up for less than a tin of dog food. But it's not over yet. Remember – no house, no TV deal." She looked shiftily at the disapproving crowds. "But you're right about one thing – *nobody* stops a Sockpuppet."

The auctioneer began. "Let's start with the

house contents. I've got a lovely moose head here, seems to have a bit of pink wafer biscuit stuck in its ear, but never mind. Now, who'll give me ten pence to start?"

The ghosts and Winnie stood miserably at the entrance to the room, hoping against hope that some miracle would prevail.

"Do I hear fifty pence? Thank you, sir. Sixty pence, seventy pence, eighty pence…"

There was a lady sitting in the front row listening attentively. She had a smart bag with the print of a famous painting on it. Martin ran up to it and inspected it for anything remotely biscuity and comforting. He was sadly disappointed.

"Now, ladies and gentleman, we move to Lot 2: a small

leotard that appears to be made out of a woollen hot water bottle cover. Who'll give me twenty pence? Thank you, madam…"

"I recognize the picture on that lady's bag," whispered Martin. "Isn't it the one we saw on the antiques programme that time when Winnie was having a meltdown?"

"Is it?" said Knitbone, fretting and glancing distractedly at the bag. "So it is. Very nice, I'm sure."

"Thirty pence…forty pence…fifty pence…"

"Yes," said Gabriel, folding his wings smugly. "But it's nowhere near as nice as ours."

Knitbone looked at Gabriel blankly. "What are you talking about?"

"Well, a while after we watched that episode, I remembered that dear old Vincent did a few paintings when he was here and left them in the back attic. Really smashing: stars and sunflowers and swirls. Would've looked lovely with the library curtains. This Krispin business made me forget all about it. Still, never mind," he sighed wistfully. "Making the library look smart is the least of our worries at the moment." Gabriel craned his neck to be able to see the proceedings.

Knitbone stared open-mouthed, reeling with shock. "Gabriel Pepper, let me get this straight. Are you trying to tell me that we have a *real, genuine, incredibly rare* painting by the famous artist, Vincent Van Fluff, tucked away in the back attic?"

"Oh no, of course not, you silly-billy."

"Oh."

"We've got fourteen."

Looking at Gabriel's innocent expression staring back at him, Knitbone marvelled at the fact that being well-read was no guarantee of being blessed with common sense. He nudged Winnie's leg firmly with his nose and barked, "FOLLOW US – NOW."

They followed Gabriel as he waddled up the stairs to the abandoned back attic. From the state of the cobwebs, it looked like no one had been up here for a very long time. On the far side stood a big trunk, covered in an old dust sheet. Gabriel dragged it off with his beak, revealing a stack of paintings.

"These are very nice," said Winnie, patiently browsing through the canvases, "but we really should get back to the auction." She held one up. It was very good. It had a bright blue sky and a vibrant yellow cornfield. "They look sort of familiar…" She noticed the signature in the bottom right-hand corner. She read it once, then three more times before she understood what she was looking at. She whistled through her teeth. "This says Vincent Van Fluff! The one who cut his ear off? I've done him at school! But…but these must surely be worth a fortune?!"

As she said the words, a world of possibility opened up before her, like the sun stepping out from behind a cloud. She drew all of the Beloveds up in a big candyfloss group hug. "You clever, smashing spooks! You brilliant, FABULOUS phantoms! We might still be in time to save Starcross yet…"

Chapter 20

Artful Dodging

The auctioneer looked down at his list. "Now, ladies and gentlemen, we come to Lot 15 – the jewel in the crown, Starcross Hall." Nora smoothed down her frazzled hair and Krispin's eyes sparkled with greed. "Let's begin at one pound, shall we?"

Krispin thrust his auction card into the air and nodded his shiny bald head eagerly.

Nobody else raised a hand. Lord Pepper blew his nose loudly in his hanky and stared at the floor.

Disappointed, the auctioneer looked about the crowd. "Only one bidder for the house? Well, that's very surprising. I know it's had some bad publicity but one pound is criminally low! Really? Just the one bidder?" He sighed. "So be it. One pound it is then, to the gentleman with the bald head, going… going…"

"One million pounds!" shouted a bold voice from the back of the room. Everyone turned to look. A girl stood on a chair, holding her hand in the air. She was wearing a costume helmet.

"Winifred Clementine Violet Araminta Pepper!"

shrieked Lady Pepper. "What do you think you're doing? Get down at once!"

Nora glared fiercely at Winnie. What was the kid playing at? She knew for a fact that the Peppers hadn't got two pennies to rub together, never mind a million pounds. Krispin was seething. How dare she? He HAD to have the house – at any cost.

Krispin raised his hand again, waving his auction card angrily. "One and a half million." There was a sharp intake of breath from the crowd.

"One and a half million to the couple in black." The auctioneer was getting visibly excited. Nora was starting to sweat and a vein on her temple was bulging in an "ambulance" sort of way.

"TWO million," shouted Winnie, without hesitation.

"Two million pounds," cried the auctioneer. "Do I hear three?"

Trembling with fury, Krispin stabbed his hand into the air again, blind to the consequences. Nora elbowed him sharply in the ribs. "What are you *doing*? We've only got two million! Have you lost your mind?" But it was too late. He was mad with longing.

"*THREE million pounds!*" screeched the auctioneer. "Unbelievable! At *three million* to the man in black, Starcross Hall is going…"

"NINE MILLION!" yelled Winnie, punching the air in triumph. Krispin deflated like a day-old party balloon and began to sob on Nora's padded jacket shoulder.

Purple with emotion, his eyes nearly popping out of their sockets, the auctioneer stood holding the gavel above his head. "At NINE MILLION pounds, Starcross Hall, of Bartonshire, England is going…going…*GONE!*" The crowd got to their feet and cheered as he smashed the gavel down with great finality and pointed to the back of the room. *"To the young lady in the helmet!"*

Chapter 21

Rest In Peace

The paintings sold for thirty-two million pounds and seventy-four pence. The papers said it was simply the greatest art discovery in history EVER.

After Winnie spoke to the police, Nora was dragged away by the local Fraud Squad, still clinging to her council desk. It seemed that the debt had only ever been ten pounds and seventy-five pence, not one million after all. Nora was packed off to Bartonshire Town Jail, her furious wails drowning out the sirens. Her little brother, Krispin O'Mystery, disappeared as if by magic.

Lord and Lady Pepper, ever the peacemakers, sent Nora some Starcross honey and mega-marrows to cheer her up. For some reason, this made Nora so angry that she smashed her prison chair to smithereens.

All the extra cash came in very handy. Once they'd paid off the (pleasingly small) council debt, there was plenty of money left over. Starcross Hall had a lick of paint and some of its more rustic features were smartened up. It goes without saying that the Peppers bought a whole room of new hats. And they turned a spare staircase into a helter-skelter, as it was a much more practical solution to getting downstairs (and was sure to come in handy for the next Starcross Banister Helter-skelter Championship).

Lord Pepper bought a new hive for his bees

and Lady Pepper replaced the ancient stove in the kitchen with a smart new gas cooker and discovered a talent for baking.

There was talk of replacing the old bath, but a family of wild ducks moved in, making this out of the question.

The most important fact was that future generations of Peppers would never be at risk of losing Starcross Hall again. There would be Peppers at Starcross – both dead and alive – for forever and a day.

It was a beautiful sunny day and Winnie lay on her back in the orchard, bees buzzing lazily about overhead. "Remember, they don't like being sucked, honey-flavoured humbugs or not."

Knitbone reluctantly spat the bumblebee out and watched it buzz and splutter angrily away.

Gabriel and Valentine were stuck into a fierce game of snap whilst Martin snoozed peacefully in the grass, dreaming of ginger biscuits, pink apple blossom settling around him. Orlando plaited daisies into Winnie's hair and sang a ladle lullaby.

Knitbone couldn't believe his luck. His wag was in the bag. He felt completely happy at last, knowing that his friends were dead special. Paw on heart, he wouldn't swap them for all the stars in Heaven.

The
End

(for now)

Meet the Author

Claire Barker is an author, even though she has terrible handwriting. When she's not busy doing this, she spends her days wrestling sheep, battling through nettle patches and catching rogue chickens. She used to live on narrowboats but now lives with her delightful family and an assortment of animals on a small, unruly farm in deepest, darkest Devon.

Meet the Illustrator

Ross Collins is the illustrator of over a hundred books, and the author of a dozen more. Some of his books have won shiny prizes which he keeps in a box in Swaziland. The National Theatre's adaptation of his book "The Elephantom" was rather good, with puppets and music and stuff. Ross lives in Glasgow with a strange woman and a stupid dog.

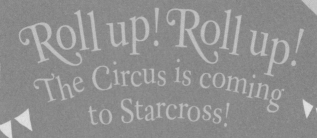

Roll up! Roll up!
The Circus is coming to Starcross!

Knitbone Pepper, ghost dog, and his furry and feathered Beloved animal friends can't wait for Circus Tombellini to pitch their big top at Starcross Hall.

But amidst the magicians, the acrobats and clowns, Knitbone senses something beastly prowling in the shadows of the circus...

ISBN 9781409580386

www.usborne.com/fiction

Knitbone Pepper

Book 2 Coming Spring 2016

By Claire Barker   Illustrated by Ross Collins

First published in the UK in 2015 by Usborne Publishing Ltd., Usborne House,
83-85 Saffron Hill, London EC1N 8RT, England. www.usborne.com

A CIP catalogue record for this book is available from the British Library.

JFMA JJASOND/15

ISBN 9781409580379 03254/1
Printed in China.